37451889

Wε Interrupt
This Broadcast

Jane da Silva novels:

Cold Smoked
Electric City
Amateur Night
A Hopeless Case

Also by K. K. Beck:

Death in a Deck Chair
Murder in a Mummy Case
The Body in the Volvo
Young Mrs. Cavendish and the Kaiser's Men
Unwanted Attentions
Peril Under the Palms

K.K.BECK

We Interrupt This Broadcast

THE MYSTERIOUS PRESS

Published by Warner Books

A Time Warner Company

M
c.1

 Mysterious Press books are published by Warner Books,
Inc., 1271 Avenue of the Americas, New York, NY 10020.

Visit our Web site at http://warnerbooks.com

 A Time Warner Company

The Mysterious Press name and logo are registered trademarks of Warner Books, Inc.

Printed in the United States of America

First printing: November 1997

10 9 8 7 6 5 4 3 2 1

Library of Congress Cataloging-in-Publication Data
Beck, K. K.
    We interrupt this broadcast / K.K. Beck.
      p. cm.
    ISBN 0-89296-642-4
    I. Title.
    PS3552.E248W4   1997
    813'.54—dc21
                                         97-34456
                                            CIP

We Interrupt This Broadcast

CHAPTER ONE

"We have a little schedule change for you, night owls," said Bob, breathing heavily into the mike and enjoying the sound of his own voice through the headphones. "We had scheduled a medley of Viennese waltzes, but as a special treat for a special person, we'll hear instead Ravel's *Bolero* here on Seattle's Classic KLEG." As was customary, he pronounced the call letters as one word.

Bob glanced over at Melanie in the corner of the broadcast booth. She was perched on a tall stool, her heels hooked over the top rung. She opened her mouth as if to say something, but he gave her a stern look and held his finger to his lips in a *shhh* gesture. Horrified, she clapped her hand over her mouth and blushed.

Bob gave her a reassuring smile. She had a hefty body, poured into a short black dress. Heft was fine with Bob. He liked something to grab on to. He imagined she was about forty-five, but well preserved.

Bob himself was pushing sixty and looked ten years older. He never gave any thought to his appearance, apart from getting a cheap haircut every couple of months and occasionally brushing the dandruff off his shoulders. His voice, however, a golden baritone dripping with testosterone, was ever youthful. Bob had learned many years ago that women were suckers for a nice set of pipes.

Up on the high stool in that short dress, there was no way Melanie could hide those ample but firm-looking thighs. She smiled back a little nervously, wriggled, and tugged at her hem, a sign perhaps that she had noticed he was looking up her skirt.

He transferred his gaze to the liner notes in front of him. "An interesting thing about this work," he began, then paused pregnantly, scanning for some esoteric bit of information to offer his listeners. Seconds ticked by as he failed to find anything suitable, then he blurted out "is that Ravel was a Basque on his mother's side."

Let's face it, he thought. I'm distracted. Bob had barely been able to contain his joy that Melanie had not only called the listener request line again tonight but had accepted his invitation to come down for a tour of the station. This was his reward for the last time she'd called, when he'd listened so patiently and with such sensitivity to her whining through an entire Schubert symphony about how tough her divorce had been.

"Let's listen to it now, shall we, night owls? In this *superb* recording on the Deutsche Grammophon label, with the Berlin Philharmonic Orchestra under the direction of Herbert von Karajan."

Melanie mouthed "Can I talk now?" twirling one of her strawlike curls on her forefinger. She had a lot of bright blond hair in a large perm.

"Sure," he said, turning down *Bolero* and removing his headphones.

"So who's the special person?" she asked.

"You, of course, my dear," he said tenderly.

She looked confused. "But I never said I liked this piece. I've never heard it before."

"Ah," he said. He threw in another pause and laid the headphones down on the console. "But this piece has a running time of an hour." Actually, it was sixteen minutes, but Bob had programmed it to repeat indefinitely. *Bolero* sounded like the same phrase over and over again anyway. And it was supposed to be sexy. "There just happens to be a bottle of champagne in the fridge in the break room. Not very good champagne, I'm afraid, but it will have to do." He gave a self-deprecating little laugh, as if to imply he was used to the good stuff. "We can use the time to relax and get acquainted. Not that I don't feel I already know you from all our wonderful phone conversations."

The champagne was Korbel from the chilled section at the twenty-four-hour convenience store nearby. After Melanie had told him it would take her about forty minutes to drive down to the station from Edmonds, a suburb to the north, Bob had thrown on Saint-Saëns's *Carnival of the Animals*, running time twenty-two minutes, and dashed across Highway 99 to make his purchase. He had also picked up a bottle of Scope mouthwash and a state lottery ticket. "I'm feeling lucky," he'd said to the Korean clerk watching *The Montel Williams Show* on the tiny TV behind the counter.

"I'm afraid it's not very glamorous," Bob said now as he guided his guest out of the studio and down the hall to the break room, a hand placed lightly on her shoulder. Things were definitely looking good. She wasn't flinching at his touch. "Radio is all illusion—that's the beauty of it."

"Gosh, it's not how I imagined it," she said, hesitating at the door and blinking as the fluorescent tubing overhead sputtered into action. The sickly glare washed over the avocado-colored fridge, the plastic wood table with cigarette burns and copies of *Gramophone, Opera News,* and *People,* and three of the kind of white plastic lawn chairs displayed in stacks at hardware stores.

Hunkering low along the far wall was the dingy beige tweed sofa. Bob's penultimate goal was to maneuver Melanie onto this article of furniture. After that, before the final chords of the final performance of *Bolero,* he hoped to exploit its Hide-A-Bed feature and proceed to his own thrilling finale. He knew from grim experience that the sofa by itself was simply too narrow. There'd been that awful time when he'd thrown out his back with that little schoolteacher from Burien. He'd had to crawl to the broadcast booth on all fours in excruciating pain to do the back-announce on this very same piece, then ad-lib a spot for, ironically, a chiropractic clinic.

He sidled over to the fridge and checked his watch as he pulled out the Korbel. "I was awfully worried about you after our last talk," he said. "But I sense that you're coming more and more to grips with the divorce. You seem ready to put the grieving behind you, get on with life, begin it anew. Who knows what life has in store for you? It's a time to be open! Receptive! Spontaneous!" He turned and popped the champagne cork, which shot into the ceiling, slightly dislodging one of the yellowed Styrofoam panels from its metal grid, as the Ravel swelled.

Franklin Payne sipped Spanish champagne and tried not to look openly hostile as his sister took the lectern. Caroline had promised him that the whole wretched thing would be over by ten-thirty at the latest.

He was hanging back in the darker shadows of the banquet room at one of Seattle's better hotels, and after having ascertained that there were no interesting-looking women at the gathering, was skittishly avoiding eye contact with anyone. He knew what these vultures were like.

Franklin was forty-two, a little on the burly side, well tailored and immaculately barbered. He had spent a lifetime repressing open hostility to Caroline, and his face had a tight, controlled look as a result.

"This evening is the culmination of a dream," Caroline began. "A dream my mother had and which my brother and I feel privileged to make into a dream-come-true—the first annual Marjorie Klegg Payne Awards for Outstanding Achievement by Local Artists." Caroline was clearly in her element and looked about as attractive as she ever did. Franklin's sister was fourteen years older, leaner and more sinewy, with pepper-and-salt hair cut in straight bangs across her forehead. Her tanned, lined face was blotched by the sun after many years of golf and tennis. Her prominent teeth and fierce, dark eyebrows gave her an aggressive look, further enhanced by her habit of wearing bristling barbaric jewelry bought at crafts fairs. Tonight, though, her enthusiasm for the spotlight had given her face a happy glow, and instead of some of the more threatening items from her jewelry box she had chosen Mom's old pearls to wear with her gray chiffon dress.

Seeing her at her best, Franklin was wary. Her habit of marrying fortune-hunting artists had cost the family plenty over the years. There had been three of them: a bad poet, a bad musician and a bad actor. The office of consort was presently vacant. A venue like this was crawling with just the kind of weasel who might lure Caroline into his greedy clutches.

Franklin had wanted to mail the award winners a check, but no, Caroline had to make a big deal out of it as usual and put together this ceremony. It wasn't bad enough that Franklin had to turn over a sizable chunk of family money to a lot of no-talent pseuds; he had to mingle with them socially as well.

He eyed a troop of starving artists and a group even lower in his estimation, low-paid arts administrators, all snuffling eagerly around the bar and buffet. Why not just get a trough for the greedy hordes and set it up in the middle of the room? God, Franklin hated artists.

Caroline was now thanking the distinguished committee who had selected the winners. They were a distinguished group all right. Distinguished by bad judgment—old hacks who'd floated around the arts scene for years with some loony faculty members from local universities thrown in to bolster the award's credibility.

The winners included an artist who glued eviscerated teddy bears and various other stuffed animals, decapitated and otherwise mutilated, onto plywood, then ran over them with her old Pontiac station wagon; a composer who had incorporated the sounds of people coughing and doors slamming into a concerto for woodwinds; and a playwright who wrote, with the aid of a dictionary, in the extinct language of an Indian tribe to which one of her ancestors had belonged. In English, the play was called *The Great Web of Life*, and was about old-growth forests.

Caroline now went on about the trophies themselves, which had been designed, at vast expense, by "an important local world-class glass artist." Caroline held one up and explained that the large pink-tinged shell-like objects were meant to represent the blossoming of the creative spirit. To Franklin, however, they looked alarmingly gynecological. When he'd pointed this out to Caroline she'd said he had a filthy mind, adding that if he were in a fulfilling relationship he wouldn't obsess like this over a fabulous piece of art. "Well, I'm not desperate enough to try to get a date with that vase just yet," he'd snapped back at her.

"Today, in this era of philistinism, when arts funding is being slashed," Caroline went on, "our family is glad to be able to provide some encouragement to those who enrich our lives with their music, their art, their poetry—those who elevate the human spirit and help make Seattle a world-class center for the arts."

That was the second time she'd used the phrase "world-class." Franklin hated that. Why should Seattle try to be world class? If people wanted world-class culture they should go to New York or London or Rome or Paris, for Christ's sake. Franklin saw no need for Seattle to have world-class baseball teams or convention centers, either. It was a vulgar conceit of newcomers to the area, and Caroline, as the descendant of pioneers, should know better.

Caroline finally wound down, but not before enraging Franklin further by mentioning KLEG-AM. "My late mother's legacy to the arts in Seattle is not limited to the award which bears her name. I'd like to take the opportunity to say that my brother and I are also committed to keeping Classic KLEG on the air, where we hope it can continue to serve as an important institution in the cultural life of our community."

How dare she speak for him like that? As far as Franklin was concerned, Classic KLEG was a money-sucking pit that served the community only as employer of last resort for a lot of pretentious geeks.

CHAPTER TWO

Zack Jordan leaned on the kitchen counter while his mother, Alice, made peanut butter sandwiches. From tiny speakers mounted high above the solid birch cabinets, *Bolero* came wafting into the airy room.

"Now that you have this job," said Zack, "do we have to listen to this stupid station all the time? At least KING-FM has normal commercials between all this classical music."

Alice sighed. "I'm just trying to familiarize myself with KLEG," she said. "I don't want to screw up."

"Are you nervous about tomorrow, Mom? Like on the first day of school?"

"Kind of. I haven't worked for thirteen years. Not since you were born." Alice wished she didn't always sound so negative. Poor Zack. It wasn't his fault that they had hit the skids so spectacularly. She tried to sound upbeat. "I hope it will be interesting and fun. And it's good for me to get out and meet people." She smiled at him tenderly. He had a cowlick that made a tuft of his fine blond hair stand up at the crown in a way she found enchanting. "Everything will be fine, darling," she said.

"Jeez, Mom. I know that," he said.

WE INTERRUPT THIS BROADCAST

Now that there were just the two of them, she wanted to make sure she didn't use Zack as a substitute adult confidant, robbing him of his childhood. The truth was, everything about KLEG depressed the hell out of her. The ramshackle studios in what looked like a shed made of corrugated tin were located in an unappealing part of south Seattle on old Highway 99. In the dusty lobby, yellowing plastic busts of Bach and Beethoven peered out from between sad-looking potted plants. The shabby, strangely unfriendly employees gave the place the look of a sheltered workshop for the marginally employable—which, she supposed, she was too.

Alice had answered lots of ads in the paper, but KLEG was the only company that asked her to come in for an interview. The ad hadn't said "sales" or "radio" at all. It described KLEG as an "important cultural resource," and the job was described as "liaising with the business community."

Her new boss, Caroline Payne Parker, was a maddeningly vague woman with huge teeth and earrings that looked like enameled ashtrays from the sixties. She had reviewed Alice's skimpy résumé, scraped together at a displaced homemakers' reentry workshop at Bellevue Community College. Alice had taught violin at the YMCA and played occasionally at weddings. She had also volunteered for various arts organizations. Caroline Payne Parker beamed and asked Alice if she wanted to sell ads for the station, perhaps as a volunteer.

Alice explained that she had a child to support, a mortgage, and a husband who had thrown over a perfectly good dental practice and run off with his hygienist, leaving her penniless. Mrs. Parker looked startled but said that, in that case, of course she could have a small salary and sales commissions, just like Ed Costello, the person who had the job now.

9

When Alice asked about the health plan, Mrs. Parker looked confused and said she was pretty sure there was one. She'd find out. "You see, we had a hired station manager for many years," she explained, "but after Mother died recently, my brother and I decided to save money by running things ourselves. I still don't know all the little niggling details."

Alice had absolutely no idea what she was expected to do, but felt that to ask for a job description would confuse and distress Mrs. Parker. The salary was pathetic, but the title, "account executive," sounded impressive, and everyone knew it was easier to find a job when you already had one. Alice Jordan had signed on with one clear goal: to get out of there and get a real job as soon as she could.

"Oh, Zack," she said to her son now, "I'm feeling kind of guilty. I'm sorry you're going to have to come home to an empty house. It's not what I ever wanted for you."

"Hey," said Zack, "if you hadn't found a job, I wouldn't have had any house to come home to. Now that you're working, can I get a virtual-reality helmet?" He glanced over at the twin lunches his mother was assembling—peanut butter sandwiches, oranges, raisins wrapped in Saran Wrap, celery sticks—"and can I start having cool stuff in my lunch again? Like Capri-Suns and Hostess Ding Dongs and Snapple? Or even Lunchables?"

Melanie was, thank God, a modern woman who pitched in and helped with the heavy lifting. Bob looked at her fondly as she struggled with her half of the Hide-A-Bed. Her dress was unzipped, with the top half hanging down from her waist and the bottom half scrunched up over her hips, revealing the shiny taupe of her control top panty hose. Her twisted dark green satin bra, unfastened in back, dangled from her strong arms by the straps and hung over her white breasts like a strand of sea-weed over the bare torso of a mermaid. Her breasts bobbed fetchingly as she struggled with the rusty mechanism. So far, all their joint efforts had produced was a shower of pistachio-nut shells.

"It seems to be stuck," she panted.

"It certainly does," said Bob, grinding his teeth and giving the thing what he hoped would be the final wrench. If this kept up, he wouldn't have enough strength to finish up before the Berlin Phil did its tenth encore.

"It's coming, God, it's coming, yes, yes," squealed Melanie in what Bob hoped was a preview of coming attractions. Just as the thing got loose and they flapped the mattress out onto the floor with a huge thud, he was startled to hear a full-throated scream floating out of Melanie's mouth. His eyes had been scrunched shut with effort, but now they flew open. Jesus, if she could get this excited just opening a Hide-A-Bed . . .

But then he realized why she was screaming. Inside the Hide-A-Bed was a large bloodstained corpse that had apparently been the cause of the jammed mechanism. It was Ed Costello, KLEG's sales manager—or rather it had been Ed Costello. There was absolutely no doubt in Bob's mind that Ed was dead. "Jesus Christ," he said, leaping backward and gagging. There was a cloying, fruity smell coming from the corpse.

Melanie, her screams reduced to panicky whimpers, rushed from the break room and ran out to the reception area, grabbing her purse. "I'm getting out of here!" she shouted.

"Yes, yes, good idea," Bob said shrilly, following her away from the thing that had been Ed. She had stuffed her breasts back into her bra, fastened it and was now jerking awkwardly at the zipper of her dress.

"Let me help you," said Bob, coming to her assistance. His voice was pitched back down in the lower register now.

"Don't touch me!" she shouted.

"Listen, I'm sure there's some sort of explanation for this," said Bob. "That was our sales manager, Ed Costello. Clearly he's met with some horrible accident." As he said this, Bob realized it would have had to be a very freaky accident indeed to result in Ed's becoming imprisoned against his will in a Hide-A-Bed. And there was all that blood, too. "I'd better call the police," he said dully.

"Don't tell anyone I was here," pleaded Melanie. "I've gotta go." She padded to the door in her stocking feet and clawed at the lock. Bob noted vaguely that she must have had shoes on when she arrived, but he didn't want to bring that up and delay her departure.

"Will you be all right?" said Bob halfheartedly. Now that the evening was clearly ruined, he was thrilled that Melanie was leaving voluntarily. "Let's keep in touch," he yelled as she slammed the door behind her.

He took a deep breath and crept back to the studio, after making sure the outer door was locked after her. Some homicidal maniac could be lurking around the darkened station. Fleetingly he hoped Melanie made it safely to her car and back to Edmonds. He shook as he reached for the phone and hit the speed-dial number for Franklin Payne, one of the station's owners.

Like everyone else in the programming department, Bob loathed Franklin Payne. Franklin's sister, Caroline, who actually held the title "station manager," was, however, a complete ditz. Some comparatively reasonable person ostensibly in authority should be notified. Bob's nerves were completely shot, but his animus for Franklin was strong enough that he was still able to enjoy the prospect of dumping a messy problem on him and ruining his evening.

"Bob Kreckelschmidt here," he said, using his real name as befitted the seriousness of the occasion.

"Who?" snapped Franklin Payne.

"Bob LeBaron, I mean. We've got a problem down here at the station."

Franklin sighed heavily. "If the transmitter is acting up again, we can wait until morning and deal with it then," he said.

"It's Ed," said Bob. "He's dead."

"What?"

"Ed's dead, I just found the body."

"What! Ed Costello?" Bob noted with satisfaction that he had Franklin's attention. He was tempted to add, "That's right, Ed Costello, your sleazy little management spy."

Bob gave a garbled account of finding Ed inside the sofa. "There's a lot of blood," he added with a certain relish.

"Are the police there?" demanded Franklin.

"No. I haven't called them yet," Bob said smarmily. "I thought you'd want to know first." That would probably give him points. These slick corporate types liked to begin damage control right away.

"For Christ's sake, Bob, call the cops. It's what you're supposed to do when you find a dead body. Dial nine-one-one. Okay? And don't touch anything. Just stay in the booth and call the police. Never mind. I'll do it. Just stay where you are."

"Okay," said Bob, sounding slightly hurt.

"I guess I'm coming down there," said Franklin wearily. "Listen, Bob, don't call my sister. She'll just get upset."

As soon as Bob hung up, he crept back into the break room.

Bolero kicked in for another sixteen minutes. Avoiding looking at Ed's body, he retrieved the half bottle of Korbel and scuttled away. Getting rid of that bottle seemed like the sensible thing to do, seeing as Bob had already been warned twice about drinking on shift. He went into the reception area and collapsed wearily into a chair, tilting the bottle to his lips and draining it methodically. How was he going to explain what had possessed him to open the Hide-A-Bed? He gazed dully at the empty bottle in his hand. He went over to Ed's messy cubicle, which the new girl they'd hired hadn't started fixing up yet, and buried the bottle under some papers in the wastebasket.

He proceeded back to the booth, slid behind the console and put on the headphones, leaving one ear half uncovered so he could hear if any killers were lurking around. He switched on the mike, activating the On Air sign. "Bob LeBaron, with you until midnight," he said. "Then, of course, it's Teresa, Queen of the Night, to keep you company till dawn. We've just heard Ravel's *Bolero*. Hypnotic, isn't it, folks?" As always, Bob felt more secure now that he was back on the air. The soothing sound of his own voice calmed him.

He consulted the log and scanned Ed's copy from the black plastic three-ring binder on the desk. "You know, friends," it read, "none of us are getting any younger." Here Ed had typed in "Chuckle" in parentheses. "I'd like to tell you about a remarkable breakthrough in mattress technology that makes a good night's sleep possible once again."

Ed had insisted Bob read this as a personal testimonial. Well, the hell with that. Ed wasn't around now to jump on him. Bob changed the lead. "You know," he began, "like many people, I've been concerned about an elderly relative who, because of the natural process of aging, had trouble getting a good night's sleep. Now, thanks to a remarkable breakthrough in mattress technology . . ."

He heard sirens approaching and reached over to close the studio door. The cops, of course, would just have to wait until he got into the Tchaikovsky *Serenade for Strings*, Opus 48, before he could let them in. Bob might have screwed up a lot during his long, down-spiraling broadcast career, but he'd never screwed up on the air.

Now that he'd overcome the physical horror of it, he reflected on the fact that Ed Costello's death, while superficially tragic, was good for KLEG and bad for its greedy, ruthless owners. In fact, Bob was quite certain that the staff would be delighted to hear Ed was dead.

CHAPTER THREE

By the time Franklin Payne's vintage Mercedes made it down to the station and crunched into the gravel parking lot, the place was surrounded by police cars. Their radios crackled in the night air. To his horror, a TV news van with a big satellite dish on top of it was rolling into the parking lot. A female police officer with dark, shiny hair coiled up in a big braid approached him. She carried a huge flashlight.

He introduced himself as one of the owners of the station. "The night man called and told me what happened," he said. "If there's anything I can do to help . . ."

"We appreciate that," she said. "The detectives are on their way. They'll probably have some questions for you." She gestured toward the news van. "Want to talk to these guys?" she said. "You don't have to."

"Hell, no," said Franklin. He loathed all local TV news on principle. He was also extremely reluctant to be identified publicly as one of the owners of KLEG. As far as he was concerned, it was akin to being exposed as the absentee landlord of a fire-trap slum tenement.

"You'll keep them out of here, I trust," said Franklin.

The officer smiled and nodded. "You bet," she said. She lifted some yellow crime-scene tape that had been attached across the front door, waited for him to duck underneath, and followed him.

From the lobby, Franklin glanced sideways into the break room. He saw two uniformed officers staring down at the open Hide-A-Bed, their broad blue backs mercifully obscuring his view of Ed. Franklin, while he had been dimly aware of a repulsive old sofa in the break room, hadn't realized it opened into a bed, but he was hardly surprised. It was typical of the slackers on the KLEG payroll to have installed a place to crash out on the job.

"These things can be a real bitch," said one of the officers. "We have to sleep on one when we visit my brother-in-law in Arizona. It's always full of Ritz crackers and shit, and there's this metal bar that gets me right in the middle of my back through this thin little mattress."

"Bummer," said cop number two.

"I'm going to ask you not to touch anything," said the woman officer, shooing Franklin through the open area surrounded by cubicles. "In fact, we'd like you to wait in here with Mr. LeBaron until the detectives arrive, okay?"

She opened the studio door and gestured inside. Bob LeBaron was sitting there behind the mike, biting his nails. Franklin hoped the detectives arrived soon. Following a time-honored radio tradition, Bob, the most obnoxious announcer on staff, had been assigned the six to midnight shift just so that no one else would have to deal with him in person. Now Franklin was being shut up with him in this little glassed-in room for God knew how long. He began to wish Caroline had been the one to have been rousted out of bed.

"The audience doesn't suspect a thing," said Bob. "I've managed to keep the flow going, and my voice didn't even tense up or anything. I thought you'd like to know. We didn't miss any spots, either."

"That's great, Bob," said Franklin, sitting down on a tall, uncomfortable stool. "You're a real pro. I'm sure Ed would be pleased to know we didn't have to do any make-goods because of his untimely death."

Bob looked hurt and confused. Franklin sighed. "Yes, I was being sarcastic, Bob," he said patiently. "Sorry, but I'm a little shook up. I never expected anything like this. Do the police know what happened?"

"They haven't told me a thing, except that it looks like he was shot and they think he might have been there for a few days." Ed narrowed his eyes. "I wouldn't rule out foul play."

"Gee, Bob, I'd say that's a pretty good bet," said Franklin, who couldn't imagine Ed accidentally shooting himself then folding himself up into a Hide-A-Bed and quietly bleeding to death. "By the way, how did you happen to actually find him?"

"Well, I had an awfully long piece running, and I'm afraid my back has been acting up again. The doctor says lying flat is the very best thing to do for it." To indicate major pain, Bob winced and lifted one shoulder a few times. "Years of huddling over microphones has really played hell with my back," he said. "You see the disks in my spine—"

"Yeah, yeah." Franklin cut him off. The last thing he wanted was a big litany of job-related medical complaints. He could well imagine years of workmen's compensation hearings, costly litigation, and support checks. He shook his head slowly. "Poor old Ed. He was a useless bastard in many ways, but no one deserves this."

"Yeah," said Bob, checking the timing on the Tchaikovsky. The digital readout indicated the piece had another ten minutes to go. "He'd been in this business almost as long as I had. We worked together years ago at KZZ. Before radio got screwed up. It was personality radio. I was the morning man, he was in sales. God, we had the best numbers in town. The dough was just rolling in." Bob's eyes started misting up. Franklin assumed Bob was mourning his vanished glory rather than his dead colleague.

"It was just a couple of years after the World's Fair. Seattle was a great town then, full of youth and vigor and promise. God, we were so young."

Bob gave Franklin a crafty look and added, "Of course, now that I'm older I'm sure glad they have laws against age discrimination. It's terrible the way some of my old pals have been thrown out on their ass in later years, but some of them have collected pretty big settlements for age discrimination."

Here was another of Bob's favorite topics. Franklin imagined he had the paperwork for such a suit all ready to file in case the ax fell.

"Anyway," Bob continued, "we used to go out and take the clients to lunch at Trader Vic's. The expense account was bottomless. I remember this little Oriental gal that used to work in the bar there, always had an orchid over her left ear. Well, whenever we walked in the place, this little gal, Michiko her name was—"

A man's face appeared at the window, followed by a timid knock cutting off the mai tai–tinged reminiscence. Franklin opened the studio door. The man was tall and lean with prematurely gray hair. He stood there looking nervously up at the On Air sign.

"It's okay," said Franklin. "He doesn't go back on the air for another ten minutes or so. I'm Franklin Payne, one of the owners."

"Detective Lukowski." He shook Franklin's hand, then looked inquiringly at Bob.

"This is Bob LeBaron, the announcer who found the body," said Franklin.

"Can we talk here?" said Lukowski.

"Why don't we go into my sister's office, the one with the sliding glass door. It's less crowded." Franklin always felt slightly claustrophobic in the studio. Even as a child, he'd hated it in here.

"Fine."

"I've got to back-announce this, then get into the all-night show," said Bob. "Okay if I come join you in about ten minutes?"

"Sure," said Lukowski, who had now been joined by another detective, older and beefier, who wore a loud sport jacket and was introduced as Detective MacNab.

The station had now become a hive of activity. Photographic flashes were coming from the break room. The place was crawling with police officers and civilians, all working away. If only the regular staff could manage to look so productive. Franklin led the two men into Caroline's office, and they all sat down.

"I know this has been a real shock," said MacNab.

"It sure has. Can you tell me what happened to Ed?"

"He was shot. That's about all we know for now."

"Here?"

"Looks like it," said Lukowski. "Your announcer told the officers who arrived first that the victim's name was Ed Costello. What type of work did Mr. Costello do here?"

"He sold ads."

"Did you supervise him?"

"No, my sister did. Nominally. Actually, no one really supervised Ed Costello. He worked mostly on commission and kept his own odd hours." Ed had met the basic minimum requirements for his job as radio time salesperson: he owned a necktie and a car. Franklin had often wondered how Ed survived on the tiny commission checks the station paid him. Maybe his wife had a real job. "In fact, we hardly ever saw the guy, and he didn't seem to be trying to drum up business, so we decided to fire him as soon as we found a replacement, which we did this week."

"So you're saying he was fired?"

"Well, we planned to fire him. We would have if we could have located him. He stopped coming to work about three days ago. Caroline called his home, but his wife didn't know where he was either."

"His wife? Has anyone told her about this?"

"I certainly haven't. I've never actually met her." The last thing Franklin wanted to do was notify the next of kin. Surely the police would do that. "I'm afraid I don't know very much about the staff or the day-to-day operations. My mother owned this station. Kind of a hobby, really. She was very fond of classical music. When she died six months ago, my sister and I inherited KLEG. Caroline, that's my sister, has been managing it since our mother's death. I'm afraid I'm not really much help."

"How about an address? Got a good address for Mr. Costello? His driver's license has a P.O. box."

Franklin reached for Caroline's address file and began fumbling through it. The fact that it wasn't in alphabetical order made the task somewhat laborious.

"Did he have any enemies you might know of?" said Lukowski.

"Well, the programming and the sales side of the house are

21

traditionally antagonistic. I get the impression there's a lot of office politics going on here all the time. Bob might know more, though of course the night-shift guy is usually out of the loop."

"When was Mr. Costello last seen at work?" asked Lukowski.

"To tell you the truth," said Franklin, "I was out of town, at my family's old summer place on Lake Crescent. I was going through some of my mother's things there, as part of settling her estate, and doing a little fishing. There's no phone there, so I've been incommunicado for a few days."

Franklin finally managed to produce a dog-eared address card. Ed apparently lived in suburban Bellevue, on what sounded like a quiet residential street. Somehow Franklin had imagined him living in a cheap walk-up apartment somewhere, with naked lightbulbs, cracked Scotch tape on the blinds and the smell of cats and cooked cabbage in the threadbare lobby. His suits were clearly of ancient vintage—left over no doubt from his glory days with KZZ—and on the rare occasions when he made sales calls he drove an old beater that Franklin hoped he parked around the corner out of view of the clients.

"Did his wife phone here, looking for him?" asked Lukowski.

"I don't know. Caroline said she didn't seem too concerned about his disappearing. The truth was, I thought he was on a bender." Most of Caroline's hires were people rendered dysfunctional by a stubborn devotion to the arts, paired with massive lack of talent. Occasionally she hired someone whose life was a mess because of simple neurosis or substance abuse. Franklin had always suspected that Ed's lack of productivity could be chalked up to booze. It was the only explanation he could come up with.

"Can you show us which desk was Mr. Costello's?" said Mac-Nab.

Franklin led them to Ed's cubicle. The desk was covered with little Post-it notes with scribbled phone numbers as well as a few blank advertising contracts, a stack of rate cards, file folders and Xerox copies of pages from ratings books. It seemed like a lot of paperwork for the few accounts Ed carried.

There was also a half-empty coffee cup with three circles of blue-green mold floating on the surface and an ancient phone-answering machine in plastic wood.

A red light on Ed's phone lit up. After a few blips, they heard the sound of tape hissing through the answering machine's insides. MacNab leaned over and turned a black knob marked *volume.*

Now they were listening to a woman's voice, a sexy woman's voice, a low purr. "Hi there, sports fans!" it said. "Tired of striking out or fumbling at third? Well, forget the bush leagues and step up to the majors. You've reached the Home Run Escort Service. Our very satisfied customers haven't struck out yet. We've got lots of lovely young ladies ready to let you slide right into home or take you on a run around all the bases. Just leave your name and number, and we'll be happy to put you on the roster for the game of your life. We'll get right back to you." Here the voice produced a feline growl of passion and then in businesslike tones added, "Visa and MasterCard gladly accepted. Sorry, no switch-hitters."

"Jesus Christ!" said Franklin. The voice on the answering machine sounded vaguely familiar.

After the beep, a male voice with bar noises in the background came on the line. "Hi, Ed," it said. "This is Gil. I've got a couple of customers over here from Osaka, and we'd like to get a little party together for them at the Sea-Tac Excelsior over by the airport. Three girls, preferably wholesome-looking blondes with big tits. If you can get Candy, that would be great, and tell her to bring the tool kit. And, Ed, get back to me right away, will you? These guys are kind of jet-lagged. Catch ya later, buddy. Use my beeper number."

They stood there in silence for a second while Bob's golden voice floated into the office from one of the big speakers in the corner. "So it's so long for tonight. Gosh, I've enjoyed keeping company with you. Get ready now for Teresa, Queen of the Night. Take it away, Teresa."

Teresa's intro theme from the second act of *The Magic Flute* came on, the spectacular coloratura passage from the Queen of the Night's aria.

Lukowski turned to Franklin and said in a deadpan voice, "You said you weren't familiar with the station's day-to-day operations. Were you familiar with the nighttime activities around here?"

Franklin was getting slightly red in the face. "God, no! This was clearly that slimeball Ed Costello's criminal enterprise. He wasn't even, strictly speaking, an employee. He was just on commission. No one else around here had any knowledge of any of this, I can guarantee it!"

Teresa's throaty tones floated into the room. "Thanks, Bob. And hello, all you denizens of the night. As my regular listeners will realize, the reason I love music so much is that it is the most sensual of the arts—the most erotic, if you like. Mmmmm, and I do. To prove my point, relax, lie down, make yourself comfortable, dim the lights, maybe throw that red chiffon scarf over the bedside lamp, as I have done here in the studio, and wallow with me in a selection of my favorite Chopin nocturnes here in an exceptionally beautiful recording with Maria João Pines."

Oh, shut up and play the music, thought Franklin. He hated

Teresa, Queen of the Night, and her sleazy patter. Unfortunately, hers was the only day part that even showed up in the ratings book, and the only profitable shift in the schedule.

"Hey!" said MacNab. "That's the same voice!"

Franklin realized he was right. Teresa, pitching the charms of hookers for the Home Run Escort Service, had used a more upbeat tone, but it was the same voice, all right.

"Where's Teresa?" demanded MacNab.

"Beats me," said Bob. "She's on tape."

"Well, we need to talk to her."

"That will be rather difficult," said Franklin, realizing that what he was going to say would make him sound even more incredibly stupid and ignorant of what went on at this ghastly radio station than he did already. "She just sends us the tapes, and we mail her a check every month. To a P.O. box. I know my sister has tried to get her to do some publicity for us, but Teresa hasn't been forthcoming. Of course I'll make every effort to locate her. She isn't, strictly speaking, an employee either, actually."

A man in khaki trousers and a plaid shirt came over with a big plastic bag containing a pair of women's black pumps with very high heels. He held the bag up to the detectives. "Found these under the couch," he said.

"Oh, hell," said Bob. Franklin looked over at him sharply.

"Maybe they belong to one of the hookers who worked out of here," said MacNab. "Let me know if you find a toolbox."

"God, I hate this place," said Franklin to no one in particular.

CHAPTER FOUR

Franklin spent the next hours huddled in his sister's office worrying about criminal liability and watching people come and go, including the late Ed Costello, now strapped to a gurney. Later, two men came and carried away the sofa bed too. Some vice detectives showed up and grilled Franklin about the Home Run Escort Service. "I had sort of wondered what Ed lived on," he told them. "I had no idea he was running whores out of here. Jesus Christ!" He hoped his sense of outrage indicated his innocence. He thought about calling one of the criminal attorneys at his firm—Franklin himself was a zoning lawyer—but decided against it.

Watching the police boxing up the contents of Ed's desk and wastebasket, including the empty Korbel champagne bottle, Franklin thought, Good riddance. He'd have liked to see the whole place boxed up and shipped out of his life.

The only possible good that could emerge from all of this was that perhaps Caroline would now see that running an operation with a bunch of losers was a big hassle. Maybe now he'd have the nerve to come right out and say he wanted to sell the damn thing.

*　　*　　*

"Not bad for a guy scraping by on his pay from that crummy radio station," said MacNab to Lukowski as they walked up the drive toward Ed Costello's suburban house. "That escort service must have been a little gold mine." The house was a low, sprawling structure set in an immaculate garden on a large lot. A BMW was parked in the driveway. The license-plate holder said "I'd rather be shopping at Nordstrom's."

Lorraine Costello answered the door in a pale green silk bathrobe. She was a good-looking woman, Lukowski thought, and maybe fifteen years younger than her husband, whose driver's license said he was sixty. Clearly a trophy wife emeritus. Despite the fact she was wearing a bathrobe, the rest of her looked ready to meet the world. Her coppery hair was arranged in a stiff pageboy and sprayed into position, including a little wave at the temple as if a breeze had lifted it just before it was flash-frozen. Her face sported a very careful and thorough makeup job, and she wore diamond earrings. She carried a small, fluffy white dog.

Lukowski let MacNab break the news. She turned very pale and stroked the dog nervously, then led them into the living room.

Lukowski cast his eye over the ivory-colored leather upholstery, where another fluffy white dog was sleeping, the huge Oriental rug covered with dog hair, the massive glass-and-metal coffee tables, the picture window overlooking a glen of rhododendrons.

"I'm afraid we have to ask you some questions," MacNab said. "When was the last time you saw your husband?"

"Three days ago. He went to work and didn't come back. He called me from the station at eleven and said he'd be there for another hour or so."

The detectives looked at each other. Bob LeBaron left at eleven, then came Teresa's broadcast. Another employee, Phil, came in at six in the morning.

If Mrs. Costello was being truthful, it sounded very much as if Ed had been murdered three days ago between eleven and six.

"Were you worried?"

"He often worked late. In fact, he always did. At least that's what he told me." Her eyes began to fill with tears. "I just assumed there was another woman. That he was off having some fling."

She hung her head. "Strange women have called him here a couple of times. Ed always said they were advertising clients, but I knew he was lying. Once I heard him say 'Never call here again.'"

"I see," said Lukowski. "I know this is all very painful."

"And he ignored me," Mrs. Costello went on. "When I told him I wanted him to help me pick out new guest towels for the bathroom, he told me to go ahead and get whatever I wanted. He said he just didn't care. I was hurt." She sobbed. "I'd buy a new outfit and not be sure if I should keep it or take it back, and I'd try it on for him, and he'd say, 'If you like it, keep it. If you don't, take it back.'" Her lip began to tremble. "He wouldn't even go shopping with me anymore. 'Buy whatever you want,' he'd say. When we were first married, he loved to shop. Maybe he shopped with those other women."

"Mrs. Costello, it looks like your husband was running an escort service from his office at the radio station. Were you aware of that?"

Her head snapped up. "You're kidding!" she said.

"That might explain why he was working late at night and why he got phone calls from strange women."

"An escort service? Like call girls?"

"Yes. Think about it, Mrs. Costello. Your husband's boss told us he didn't make much money there. But you clearly have a very comfortable life here."

"I wondered what happened," she said in a bewildered tone. "When I married Ed years ago, he had a great job. Sales manager at KZZ. But then things kind of went downhill. Radio can be very unstable. I kept maxing out the credit cards just buying basic stuff, you know? When he ended up working at KLEG, I thought he'd hit rock bottom. It was so depressing. Instead, we were finally able to live decently and have nice things. I could fix up the house the way I wanted it." She wiped tears from her eyes and said, "He did it for me. He knew how hard it was for me having to scrimp. Poor Ed."

After a few more routine questions, the detectives made a cursory check of Ed's papers in a small study. Mrs. Costello and the dogs hovered around, and she kept murmuring "I'm afraid I don't know anything about finances."

It was pretty clear her husband hadn't kept any records from the Home Run Escort Service at the house. The previous year's tax return showed a gross income of twelve thousand dollars in salary and commissions from KLEG.

Back in the living room, MacNab said gently, "Is there someone you want to call? Someone to be with you?"

"It's okay," she said in the same vague, shocked tones she'd been using since she heard the news. "My personal trainer will be here soon. She's always there for me."

"Mrs. Costello," said Lukowski, "considering what you told us—that you suspected your husband was having an affair—we have to ask you if you were so angry that you might have wanted to harm him, or gone down to the station where he worked late and confronted him."

"What? No. I never went near the place. It was really tacky. I hardly ever go into the city, anyway."

"Can we ask where you were three nights ago?"

"Thursday?"

"Yes?"

"I was alone here. Like I am every night. I was watching the shopping channel. In fact, I think it was Thursday that I ordered a really cute tennis bracelet to cheer myself up." Her eyes glazed over with tears. "And Ed will never get to see it."

"Can you think of anyone who might have had a grudge against him?" asked Lukowski.

"No. Ed was always friendly and happy. A typical sales guy. Real outgoing. Everyone loved him. He was a great guy."

As the two men walked back to their car, MacNab said, "She may not think he was such a great guy when the IRS catches up with her."

The next morning, red-eyed and not very rested, Franklin Payne sat across the desk from his sister in her office at KLEG, and listened to her berate him. "I can't believe you didn't call me. No one tells me anything around here. Why didn't Bob LeBaron call me? I heard about it on the morning news."

"I didn't want to worry you," he said, avoiding her gaze by looking through glass doors into the outer office. Carl, the record librarian, was shuffling in. As usual, he looked as if he'd spent the night in a Dumpster and chosen his wardrobe there. Today he was wearing a matted mustard-colored acrylic cardigan, paint-stained jeans and rubber thongs. God, didn't any of these people ever wash their hair? Carl's lanky strands hung over his narrow little face like a screen.

Franklin waved at Carl through the closed glass door, and Carl gave a toss of his greasy locks and a curt nod before scuttling into the corridor leading to the record library. Franklin took grim satisfaction from the fact that the closed sliding glass door never failed to terrify the paranoid, underachieving, self-righteous leeches known collectively as the KLEG staff.

Whenever he came by the station, which he did as seldom as possible, and strode into Caroline's office, he made a big deal of sliding the door shut and returning the furtive, hostile glances of the employees with a wolfish smile through the glass. When discussing delicate matters, he always positioned himself with his back to the glass in case there were lip readers among them.

And as he left, Franklin invariably threw a loud parting remark over his shoulder, just for their benefit, as he opened the door. Something like "Remember, Caroline. Lean and mean!" or "Format change: Think about it, Caroline!" Maybe he couldn't get his sister to listen to reason, but he could at least undermine morale among the bloodsuckers.

Caroline finally wound down, and Franklin said snappishly, "I'm telling you, Caroline, this is serious. We could end up getting a lot of bad publicity. Who knows what sordid stuff will come up during the investigation? And we may have a homicidal maniac on the staff! Seeing as everyone around here is unhinged to some degree, it's not going to be easy to figure out who the bad apple is."

"Well, surely the police will figure it out," she said. "Meanwhile, I think the best thing to do is soldier on. The way Mama would have wanted it. Do we know anything about the funeral arrangements? I think we must send flowers. White is always best for funerals."

"For Christ's sake, Caroline! Ed Costello was a pimp! The cops may think we're involved. You could be a laughingstock. I can see the headlines now: 'Arts Patroness or Procuress?' Of *course* I'd like to see KLEG stay on the air forever, a living tribute to Mom's memory, making a wonderful contribution to the local arts scene. I want that as much as you do. But it may not be possible."

"Why do you always have to be so negative?" said Caroline in the grating big-sister tone of voice that always whisked Franklin back to his unhappy childhood. She clicked her tongue contemptuously. "The killer can't be anyone on the staff. After all, the police found those shoes under the sofa. They don't seem to belong to anyone here."

"For all we know, Bob LeBaron gets off wearing heels on his shift," said Franklin bitterly. "Anyway, the press is bound to descend on us at any minute. Let's at least coordinate some sort of response."

Caroline looked thoughtful. "A press release, perhaps. Maybe we can put in a little pitch for KLEG. Seattle's only AM classical station." She gazed out into the office as if seeking inspiration. Franklin began to feel a little twitch in his left eye. "Oh, look. Here's the new salesperson. I think you'll like her. She's very sweet. And she's a musician."

Great. Another underachieving artist. What they really needed was some sleazebag like Ed who could run around and pick up a few contracts to pay some of the bills. A sleazebag like Ed, but with some push. Not that Franklin wanted the station to be too successful. That would only encourage Caroline. Franklin wanted to avoid a complete hemorrhage of red ink while he looked around for someone to buy this little corner of hell. Of course, now that a dead body was linked to the place, maybe a buyer would be too much to hope for. Franklin hoped there were no more fresh horrors waiting to be discovered, but he wasn't going to bet on it.

CHAPTER FIVE

There was a feeble knock on the glass door. Judy—the receptionist, a thin-lipped fortyish woman with rounded shoulders,
scraggly, transparent hair and pale skin that revealed violet-
colored veins around the temples—cringed apologetically at the
latch. Franklin leaned over and slid open the door, scowling at
her.

He was convinced that Judy listened in on his phone calls to
his sister. He had heard ambient office noise and raspy, tuber-
cular breathing in the background, and more than once he'd received mail at the station which was presented to him taped shut
with "Opened in Error" scrawled across the front in her re-
pressed backhand.

"Alice wants to know if she can have Ed's cubicle," she said.
"You didn't tell me you'd hired her. She just showed up, and I
don't know what to do with her. Am I supposed to train her or
what? She's asking for office equipment and business cards."

Despite her Uriah Heep body language, Judy habitually emit-
ted rays of rebellious hostility from her scary light blue eyes. She
clearly felt she should do the hiring and firing. Caroline had

brushed off her brother's hints that Judy had delusions of grandeur.

"Send her in, Judy," said Caroline. "I'd like my brother to meet her."

Judy left and returned with a pleasant-looking woman in her late thirties with curly light brown hair and a rosy face. She was clearly overdressed for the KLEG office, wearing a powder-blue suit.

After being introduced and shaking hands with Alice Jordan, Franklin turned to Judy, who was hovering around in her moth-like way, and said, "Do you think we can get some coffee, or isn't that in the receptionist's job description?"

She zapped him with the hate-laser look and said, "Actually, my title is office manager."

He gave a little smirk and said to Alice, "How do you take your coffee?"

She looked startled and said, "Oh, I don't want any, thanks," and gave Judy a smile of sisterly solidarity. She clearly thought Franklin was an oppressor of women. Fine. Might as well start alienating her right away. Happy employees didn't fit in with Franklin's plans for KLEG.

"Sit down," said Caroline. "This is my brother, Franklin. He owns the station too, but he's not very interested in what we do here. I inherited my mother's interest in the arts."

"That's right," said Franklin with a big smile. "Caroline's the sensitive one. I'm boorish, materialistic and crass."

Alice sat down and gave each sibling a wary smile. "I guess I should get in touch with some of the regular advertisers," she said. "Let them know I'll be taking over for Ed."

"Oh, I think you'll find that they've heard Ed is no longer

with us," said Franklin solemnly. "The poor bastard's body was discovered shot to death here last night."

"What?" said Alice.

"Not only that, apparently he was running an escort service out of his cubicle here at the station."

Wide-eyed, Alice looked over at Caroline. Her new boss's large teeth were resting on her lower lip. She was looking down at her lap where she fiddled with a massive copper bracelet studded with beach rocks. Franklin's more pleasing features were equally inscrutable. "You're kidding, right?" Alice said.

"I wish I were," said Franklin.

Alice took a deep breath. Strangely, this bizarre state of affairs actually seemed to give her more confidence. During her many years as a suburban housewife, Alice had spent a lot of time reading true crime paperbacks and watching *Cops* and *America's Most Wanted* on TV—although she'd had to give up *Court TV* when she had the cable yanked in an economy move. Lurid crime was actually one of the few areas in which she felt she had some expertise.

"I imagine the press will be all over us anytime now," said Franklin, glancing at his watch. "Not real great publicity."

Alice heard herself saying, "I think a simple statement that says KLEG wants to get to the bottom of any crimes committed here, supports all the efforts of the appropriate law enforcement agencies, and then refers all questions to them is the best course," she said.

With an air of happy surprise, Franklin said, "That seems reasonable."

"We should say something nice about poor Ed, shouldn't we?" said Caroline. "How he was dedicated to classical music or something?"

"Was he?" said Alice with a sympathetic air.

"He was a pimp!" said Franklin. "I shudder to think what else has been going on around here on your watch, Caroline. Certainly nothing that generates legitimate revenue."

She straightened up in her chair and gave her brother a fierce look. Alice noticed him flinch.

"Look, we're all kind of stressed out," he said in an apologetic, tired voice. "I'd better get over to my office. Why don't you fax me the press release when it's done? I'd like to have a look at it."

"We let him see the legal stuff," said Caroline begrudgingly. "He's a lawyer."

After Franklin left, Caroline turned Alice over to Judy, saying vaguely, "I suppose she'll need a desk and all that."

As soon as Caroline had shut herself back up in her office, Judy put a hand on Alice's sleeve. "I suppose you can have Ed's old cubicle. The police cleaned it all out. Want a tour of the station first?"

"Sure," said Alice, who was especially interested in the crime scene. "Tell me more about Ed Costello," she added. "It must have been a terrible shock."

"Ed wasn't too well liked around here," said Judy. "We don't think he really cared about KLEG." Alice made a mental note to pretend to care about KLEG.

Judy led her down a long corridor. "We'll start with the record library." Here, in a large, dim, windowless room lined with CDs and LPs, were two facing desks lit with round bright circles from a pair of metal lamps. At one desk sat an elderly man in a checked shirt with wisps of white fluffy hair, a birdlike profile, and Coke-bottle glasses. Opposite him sat a young man with oily hair, wearing a nappy mustard-colored sweater.

Judy introduced Alice to the older man, Phil Bernard, who was apparently the program director. He rose stiffly.

"I've certainly enjoyed you on the air," said Alice. "I didn't realize you also chose the music."

Phil's features took on a look of deep contempt. "Unfortunately there are *some* members of the staff who don't know the first thing about classical music," he said. "I program their shifts, and check over the entire schedule for duplications and lacunae."

Alice looked around the room. "I see you still have a lot of LPs," she said.

Phil's head reared and his nostrils flared like a skittish horse. "If I had my way, this whole CD nonsense would never have happened. There was no need to replace vinyl. We did just fine before this stuff came on board!"

Judy interrupted his tirade. "And this is Carl Weeb, the record librarian," she said.

Alice smiled at Carl, who gave her a brief glance and an unintelligible whisper before letting his eyes drop back down to a computer keyboard.

"Oh," she said, picking up a CD sitting on the corner of Phil's desk. "The new Cecilia Bartoli."

"Oh, so you actually know something about music," said Phil skeptically. "That's usually a reason not to get hired around here."

The phone rang on Phil's desk, and he picked it up. "Record library," he said in a smooth, announcer voice.

"Think about it," he said to the caller with a sneer. "Isn't that like asking who's buried in Grant's Tomb?"

After a pause he said, "Pachelbel."

When he'd hung up, he said to Carl, "Another knucklehead

wanting to know who wrote Pachelbel's Canon in D." Carl produced a thin smile and huddled back over his keyboard.

Phil turned back to Alice and gave a snort. "I hope you don't have any tasteless stunts in mind for the staff. Ed Costello always wanted us to do remote broadcasts from used-car lots and electric organ stores!"

Alice didn't think unleashing Phil on the public was necessarily a good idea. She thought that for the good of the station's image, he and Carl should remain hidden back here in their little den.

Franklin always loved coming back to his law offices after a visit to KLEG. Here the employees gave the appearance of being functioning members of society, were reasonably well groomed and had adequate social skills. The bland, expensive decor was soothing, the view of Puget Sound and the Olympic Mountains beyond, often inspiring.

In his office he browsed through a stack of letters, faxes and phone messages, and listened to his voice mail. There were several routine calls and then something that produced a wave of horror. It was a message from Ed Costello.

"Say, listen!" Ed's voice had its usual false urgency, characteristic of the habitually desperate salesman. "I think I've got a hot buyer for the station. This guy I worked with years ago. Looking for a talk-format thing. I figure a going-nowhere AM station is just the ticket. As soon as we get together a legal finder's-fee agreement, I'll set up a meeting with my guy and his people. Believe me, this party is hot to trot."

Franklin's spirits rose, then sank again. A legitimate buyer for the station was exactly what he wanted. He'd never thought a sleazy guy like Ed would have been able to find one. But Ed had cagily failed to say who the hot prospect was, taking his secret with him to the grave.

"They removed the sofa," Judy explained to Alice as the two women stood in the break room staring at the wall where the sofa had stood. A smudgy line indicated its previous position.

"And they found him folded up inside it?" asked Alice. "How strange. What kind of a person was Ed?"

Judy's thin lips made a downturned line. "He wasn't very popular. He showed a real insensitivity to the programming department. He didn't know anything about the format." She leaned over confidentially. "And he kept saying he couldn't do a better job selling ads because the ratings were so bad. But of course our numbers are low. The kind of intelligent, sensitive listener who listens to classical music isn't going to fill out those dopey rating-book diaries. There's really nothing more pathetic than a radio time salesman," she added tactlessly.

"You can put your lunch in here," she went on, opening the refrigerator door. "But if there's meat in anything, I'd appreciate it if you don't put it on the top shelf. That's where I put my lunch, and I don't want any meat touching it. Also"—she indicated a small microwave oven, which Alice thought needed a good scrubbing—"I'd appreciate it if you never use this for any animal protein. I'm extremely sensitive, and if even the smell of dead animals gets on my food, I get ill. In fact, I have a lot of health problems, simply from living in a world where others are less particular about what they eat."

"I see," said Alice, who had decided that leaving this place for lunch, even if it meant sitting in her car on the shoulder of Highway 99, would give her a heady sense of freedom.

"We can go into the studio in just a sec," Judy said, leading

Alice back into the main office area and pointing up at the red On Air light. "Just never walk in here when that light is on."

Alice, who had been dutifully listening to the station all day long the previous week, recognized the melodious voice of Daphne Hamilton, the morning-shift announcer, coming from the office speakers. "And now," she was saying in hushed tones, "Maori diva Kiri Te Kanawa sings the Pie Jesu from Fauré's *Requiem* with the Montreal Symphony Orchestra."

As the music came up, the On Air light went out, and Judy pushed open the heavy studio door.

"Daphne, this is Alice Jordan. Caroline hired her to replace Ed."

In front of a microphone sat a thin, languid, pretty, middle-aged woman with her dark hair in a ballet dancer's chignon. She was wearing a large flowered and fringed shawl over a dress that looked as if it were made from a Pier One Indian bedspread.

"Really? Hello!" said Daphne, gazing up at Alice with liquid brown eyes. She appeared to be wearing stage makeup—orange base, two slashes of rouge at a forty-five-degree angle, kohl-rimmed eyes and a scarlet mouth. "Maybe you can do something about this dreary old place. No one knows we exist. I think you should make me a star!" She flung her long-fingered, red-tipped hands gracefully up over her head and laughed rather wildly.

"I guess I'd better take some of these calls," said Judy, glancing down at the studio phone. "All the lines seem to be lit up."

She left, and Daphne put a hand on Alice's arm. "We're playing nothing but funereal music because of Ed," she confided, with a dramatic roll of her dark eyes. "Phil thought it was respectful, even though none of us were friends with Ed or anything. I mean, radio sales guys are the lowest of the low, no

41

offense, but after all, any human life is sacred in and of itself, whatever form it takes." Daphne leaned back in her chair. "So what do you think of this place so far?"

"Well, I suppose it's not exactly normal today, what with the murder and all," ventured Alice.

"It's never really normal," said Daphne. She wiggled her long fingers in the air in front of her face and narrowed her eyes. "There are strange undercurrents here all the time, odd dramatic surges of intense emotion." Daphne looked as if she thrived in such an atmosphere.

Judy came back into the studio. "One of those calls is for you," she said to Alice. "Franklin Payne. You can take it at Ed's desk."

Alice left the studio, went over to the bare little cubicle in the outer office, and picked up the phone. Was he going to yell at her because she hadn't written the press release yet?

"Listen," said Franklin Payne. "I've been thinking about this, and I think I should go over all the stuff on Ed's desk with you. Leads and so forth. Caroline doesn't pay much attention to the sales side of the house. The first thing we should do is get all of Ed Costello's papers back from the police. They boxed everything up and carted it away. I'll call them and find out when we can have it back. We need all that stuff. I'll help you go through everything there with a fine-tooth comb. There may be some hot leads that need pursuing."

"All right," said Alice, feeling confused. She didn't like the idea of having two bosses, and she was surprised that Franklin Payne wanted to go through a bunch of files and memos with her. Caroline had already told her he wasn't too interested in the station. But he told her Caroline wasn't interested in sales. "Do you think I could ask you a few questions about exactly what I'm supposed to be doing?" she said. "I've never sold anything be-fore, and I could use a few pointers."

"All right," he said, sounding a little impatient. "Come by in about an hour. Then you can make a few calls. You need to jump right in and hit the street."

After she hung up, she decided that she'd better write that press release. She would ask Judy if there was a computer or a typewriter she could use. Over at Judy's desk she heard the pale-eyed receptionist speaking into the phone. "Sure," she was say-ing. "Bring your TV crew right down here. I'll be glad to show you where the body was and tell you all about it. I'm sort of the operations manager here."

She hung up and said, "Do you think my hair looks okay? I'm going to be on TV. All those phone messages were from the press. Three TV stations and both daily newspapers. Isn't it ex-citing?"

"Um," began Alice tentatively, "actually, Caroline and Franklin and I already discussed this, and the feeling was to keep the whole thing low key. I was asked to write a press release, re-ferring everyone to the police department."

Judy took in her breath sharply, producing a snaky little sound, and her eyes narrowed to mean little slits.

"Listen, I don't want to step on anyone's toes," Alice said quickly, realizing her voice sounded tense. "It's just that I don't re-ally understand how things operate around here, and I don't want to get in trouble on my very first day."

Caroline had drifted over to the reception area. "Trouble?" she said. "What do you mean trouble?"

"The press is on its way to cover Ed's murder," said Judy. "I volunteered to show them around. I think, as office manager, that's entirely appropriate. But Alice says you and Franklin decided to keep a lid on everything."

"Oh," said Caroline vaguely. "We did? Actually, I'd like to talk to them, too. I think it's very slack of them not to have covered the awards banquet last night. If Seattle is ever going to be the world-class arts town it should be, the media will just have to start covering important arts events."

"I'm glad to hear you aren't stonewalling," said Judy. "I believe very strongly in freedom of the press and the public's right to know." She gave Alice a self-righteous look.

"Do you still want me to write the press release?" Alice asked Caroline.

"All right," said Caroline. "Don't forget to mention the Marjorie Klegg Payne Award."

Alice had no idea what the Marjorie Klegg Payne Award was, but she wasn't about to admit it. "Do you have some information on it?" she asked. "I want to make sure I get all the details right."

"I'll write the press release," said Judy. "It'll be faster than telling you all about it." She gave Alice a sly smile of triumph.

"Maybe you should do something about your hair before the cameras get here, Judy," said Alice sweetly. "It could use a good brushing and maybe some gel on the frizzy parts."

CHAPTER SIX

Franklin was pretty confident that Alice Jordan would do a lousy job. She looked scared and genteel and not very aggressive. With any luck, working full-time, she would do as poorly as Ed had in the few idle moments when he wasn't sending prostitutes out to motels. This Jordan woman would probably get discouraged and quit, and he could try to find a more suitable person for the job, like some broken-down old used-car salesman with a little fight still left in him. Trying to train Alice Jordan was just going to be a waste of time.

But Franklin *was* interested in finding out who Ed's buyer for the station might be. If he continued to supervise Alice fairly closely, he might be able to figure it out from Ed's papers when the police returned them.

When she arrived and sat there in his office, her hands folded demurely in her lap, she said, "I have to be honest and tell you I'm not really sure how to go about this."

"No problem," said Franklin easily. "It's a piece of cake. I did it summers when I was a kid. Just find out what the client needs and sell it to them. Spend a few days calling on existing clients, and tell them you'll be handling the business. You know, a courtesy thing. Then, the ones who are off the air, ask them when they want to start advertising again.

"As soon as I get all that paperwork from Ed's desk back from that Detective Lukowski, you and I will go through it looking for leads. Then you can go out and get new business. We'll pay you double commissions on first-time business. On top of your salary." Franklin was sure that somewhere in that mountain of papers on Ed's desk was a name or a phone number that would lead him to the hot prospect willing to buy KLEG. The way he was feeling now, Franklin was interested in giving it away.

"What kind of advertisers should I be targeting?" asked Alice.

"The truth is, our ratings are terrible," he said airily. No point giving her false hope. "Let's face it, who wants to listen to classical music on AM? Most of our listeners are about a hundred years old, listening to us on old Bakelite plastic radios with glowing tubes inside. Or, if their driver's license hasn't been yanked because of inoperable cataracts, they listen to us in the antique car they've been driving for thirty years that doesn't have FM.

"Ask yourself what old people like that buy with their pensions and Social Security checks. Burial plots. Arthritis remedies. Denture adhesive. We're talking about an old demographic, no doubt about it.

"Except for Teresa's fans, of course. Don't ask me who they are. A cult following of crazed insomniacs. You'll get a feel for it."

"I see," said Alice. "Your sister says I should emphasize the contribution advertisers will be making to cultural life in Seattle." There seemed to be a strain of doubt in her voice.

"Maybe so," said Franklin, who didn't believe any such thing.

There were many charities far worthier than KLEG, which was, after all, a business, even if it wasn't run like one. "Judy should have a list of advertising agencies. Go visit their media buyers and find out who their clients are. Tell them you can offer a stable, loyal listenership of old people. And you might monitor some of the other stations on the dial. Find out who's advertising on them and rush over there and see if you can grab part of the budget."

Alice was now taking notes, something he found rather touching. Most of the staff reacted to everything he said with thinly veiled hostility or outright sneers.

"Here's another tip," he added. "Don't make appointments with the direct clients, just the ad agencies. If you phone first it's that much easier for them to brush you off."

He stood up to indicate the meeting was over. "Let me know how you're getting on," he said without enthusiasm.

"All right," said Alice. He walked her to the door of his office and opened it for her. Just then Franklin's secretary rushed into the room. "There are two women who insist on seeing you," she said in a tense voice, the white showing all around her irises. "They're making a scene in the lobby."

"Who are they?" Franklin asked.

"They say their names are Dagmar and Carmen."

Two striking young women burst past the partly open door. The tall blonde was presumably Dagmar. She had on a tight red power suit with a very short skirt and matching four-inch heels. Carmen, a Latin bombshell type, wore similarly slutty business attire in black.

"Hey! Are you Franklin Payne?" asked Dagmar belligerently, jabbing a long red fingernail at him.

"Yes," he said, looking startled. They had brought a cloud of cloying perfume with them.

"Ed Costello owed us a lot of money from credit card receipts, and I guess, seeing as you were his boss, we'll have to collect from you now."

"Don't be ridiculous," snapped Franklin. "I don't know anything about Ed Costello and his repulsive business interests."

"Bullshit," snarled Carmen, revealing dazzling white teeth. "Try and stiff us, and my boyfriend will take care of you, but good. He won't let anyone mess with me." She put both hands on her hips, a maneuver that stretched her suit jacket wide to reveal the tops of her breasts tumbling out of a black lace push-up bra.

Franklin turned to his frazzled secretary. "Get someone from security," he said calmly. She scurried out of the room. He turned back to Carmen and Dagmar. "I resent any implication that I'm some kind of a pimp. Why don't you gals get yourselves a lawyer to make a claim against Ed's estate?"

The secretary trotted back in, followed by a nervous-looking blue-uniformed guard of twenty or so with a thin mustache. He was carrying a paperback copy of a Stephen King novel, and a finger marked his page.

Franklin pointed at the two women. "Jason, will you please escort these escorts the hell out of here!" Carmen and Dagmar stood glaring at Franklin and made no sign of moving. "Or we'll have to call the real cops," he added in an icy tone. "Maybe the vice squad."

"Okay," said Dagmar. "But you haven't heard the last of us."

Alice, fascinated, followed the two women and the shy-looking security guard to the elevator. The four of them glided silently down to the main floor. Alice followed Carmen and

Dagmar out onto the sidewalk. Dagmar paused to fire up a smoke, and Alice lagged behind, pretending to remove some lint from her lapel.

Parked in the loading zone in front of the building was a flashy red Corvette with a muscular-looking man wearing sunglasses at the wheel. The two women got into the car and it peeled away from the curb, but not before Alice had memorized the license-plate number. Maybe Carmen's thuggy-looking boyfriend had already tried to collect from Ed and had ended up killing him. Before Alice did anything else, she'd call the police and give them this license number from the pay phone down the street, feeling the same heady rush she got vicariously from her true-crime paperbacks.

She remembered the detective's name. Franklin had just mentioned it. Detective Lukowski wasn't in, but she left a voice mail message, trying not to sound too breathless and excited.

The thrill of calling in a police tip had momentarily canceled out the trepidation she felt about going out and making sales calls, but now she steeled herself and drove to Queen Anne Hill.

"So no one at KLEG has ever met this Teresa?" said MacNab to his partner, Lukowski. The detectives were eating a Vietnamese lunch in a tiny downtown restaurant.

"That radio station has got to be one of the flakiest places I've ever seen," said Lukowski, shaking his head.

"They say they didn't know about the hookers. They didn't even know Costello had his own phone line. Judy explained the whole Teresa thing to me."

"The mean-looking receptionist?"

"That's right. The deal is this: Teresa mails them a tape with all the talk on it. 'You just heard blah-blah-blah,' and then that nerdy little guy, Carl—"

"The one with dirty hair?"

"That's right. He sticks in all the music from the station's library."

"Well, how do they pay her?" asked MacNab.

"They send a check to a P.O. box downtown."

"Who's the check made out to?"

"Cash. Can you believe it?"

"Who cashes the check?"

Lukowski picked up a spring roll. "Teresa Hoffman," he said. "That's her name. But no one on the staff has ever met her."

"Except Ed Costello," said MacNab.

CHAPTER SEVEN

"Ed Costello? Never heard of him."

It was a few minutes before noon, and Alice was leaning on the counter at Carlson's Clock Shop, speaking to a grizzled old man in a cardigan.

Carlson's was a small, dusty, family-owned business on Queen Anne Hill, specializing in antique clocks and repairs. It seemed like a good bet. Those older listeners Franklin had described probably had plenty of broken old clocks lying around. According to the station's records, Carlson's had been on the air for years, sponsoring something called *This Date in Music*.

"Ed Costello was your contact at KLEG," she explained, slightly rattled by the sound of masses of clocks ticking.

"KLEG. Oh, yeah. Dad used to advertise with them."

"You still do," said Alice. "And we certainly appreciate the business."

"Haven't seen anyone from there for years," said the old man. "Certainly not any Ed Costello."

"I just wanted you to know that I'll be handling the account now, and I want to make sure you're happy with the advertising and . . ." She began to trail off.

"KLEG, huh? Well, I think I'd better pass. We get good results from the Yellow Pages and the neighborhood paper. No need to be on the radio." He turned away from her and fiddled with a pair of chubby metal pinecone-shaped weights hanging from one of a half dozen cuckoo clocks in a row on the wall.

"But you *are* on the radio," said Alice, feeling the whole situation slipping away from her. "You have an annual contract."

"Well, we should cancel it," he said over his shoulder. He turned back and smiled pleasantly. "I'll have the bookkeeper look into it." Above his head, the cuckoo clocks made creaking sounds, a brace of doors flew open and horrible little wide-eyed birds flew out and started making shrill, taunting sounds. Chimes and bongs began to kick in from around the store. The old man produced a gold watch from his pocket, flipped open the lid, smiled down at it with satisfaction, then closed it up again and put it away. "Anyway," he said, his voice rising above the sound of chimes and bells and cuckoos, "word of mouth is the best advertising there is, if you ask me."

"I see. Well, thank you for your time," she said.

"We got plenty of that," he yelled over the din, with an irritating grin. Alice left the shop with as much dignity as she could muster, went out to the car and wept quietly for a few minutes, until she noticed the meter had run out.

"I was kind of hoping to find some kind of a trick book," said Lukowski sadly. He and MacNab were at Lukowski's desk, going through the box of papers from Ed's desk. "My guess is we're looking for someone from this guy's hooker business."

Ed Costello's desk had produced a dreary pile of advertising contracts, and numerous phone messages, many of which seemed to say "Called again. Wants desperately to talk about advertising. *Please* get in touch," and a file folder marked "Leads" that contained restaurant reviews, print ads torn from symphony programs, a newsletter called *Puget Sound Senior*, a chamber of commerce listing of nursing homes and funeral parlors, and a publication on rough newsprint called *Asian Dolls* that featured smudgy pictures of young women from Manila and Taipei who wanted to correspond with sincere American men, including geriatrics, marry them, and get a green card.

"Think the wife knew about his escort business and was playing dumb?" asked MacNab.

"*Playing* dumb? I thought she had your basic room-temperature IQ. She's one of those women who are only good at one thing. And that's shopping."

MacNab nodded. "Let's face it, the only reason he had that job at the radio station was to have a quiet place to do business. If the wife knew what he was up to, he'd have done it all from home. Saved himself a commute."

"We've definitely got to pursue the escort-service angle. Those are usually pretty quiet little businesses, but whenever you get vice, you can get other wonky stuff. Somehow I can't imagine those classical nerds at the radio station had it in them to blow someone away," said Lukowski. "And the wife's shopping-channel alibi will probably check out. I called them today to see when that order came in, and they're finding out."

He looked down at the papers all over his desk and sighed. "Well, let's run some of these folks through the computer and see if we come across anyone interesting." He had assembled a list of names and phone numbers from the flurry of Post-it notes and "Please call back" memos they'd found on Ed's desk.

"At the same time, I'm going to check out the tip I got on my voice mail. The one from that woman who saw those hookers try to get Franklin Payne to cough up."

Franklin was so infuriated by the visit to his office from Dagmar and Carmen that he canceled a lunch appointment and drove down to KLEG to have it out with Caroline in person. Up until now, his plan had been to line up a buyer, make it look like an unsolicited deal and get her to sign. He knew he couldn't persuade her to go along with any active efforts on his part to find a buyer. If it looked as if he had initiated a sale, she'd just dig in harder. But maybe now she'd listen to him. She *had* to listen to him.

When he got there, she was sitting in her office talking to Phil. Franklin burst in on them just in time to hear Phil say pompously, "Without more budget to get the tools we need to do the job, we can't be the best we can be."

Caroline turned to Franklin and gave him a goofy smile. "Phil has been explaining to me why the record library needs a Grove's *Dictionary of Music and Musicians*," she said. "Apparently it's rather expensive."

"About twenty-three hundred," said Phil blithely.

Franklin turned on him. "You people are lucky to have jobs," he said. "Don't push it."

"Frankie!" said Caroline.

Phil turned pale, and Franklin said, "Look, nothing personal, Phil. Just hang in there with what we've got for a while, okay? To put it bluntly, now that Ed's sex business is boarded up, this place hasn't got a single profit center. Can I interrupt here for a moment and talk to my sister?"

Phil scurried out of Caroline's office, and Franklin slid the glass door shut with a huge *blam*.

"Really!" said Caroline. "Think about morale around here, will you? These artistic types can be very touchy. You're making my job as a sensitive manager of people just that much more difficult."

"Listen, Caroline, I've had it with this place. I want you to know that a couple of bimbos in four-inch heels and very short skirts came over to my office today—my office, Caroline—and made a big scene! They said Ed owed them money from his sleazy escort business and I was supposed to pay it. I can't have this sort of thing going on! What are my partners going to think? People will laugh at me. I can't have that!"

"But those women don't have anything to do with KLEG," said Caroline in a tone of patient reasonableness. "Now that Ed's out of the picture, what's the problem?"

"Can't you see? Ed's running a string of whores out of here is symptomatic of a greater rot."

"Just because he ran an escort service doesn't mean the girls actually—"

"For Christ's sake, Caroline. Blow jobs! Ed was selling blow jobs out of here. And hookers are coming to my office. I used to joke that Ed couldn't sell pussy on a troop train, but apparently that's the one thing he could sell."

"Thank goodness Mama wasn't here to learn about it," said Caroline. She looked a little trembly and unsure of herself for once. Emboldened, Franklin leaned in closer and said, "Let's sell the place, Caroline. It's the only way. I'll run an ad in *Broadcasting* magazine. I'll get a broker on the job."

"But, Frankie, KLEG is my career. I'm a businesswoman—with a keen commitment to the arts. Mama wouldn't let me run this place. No one ever let me be in charge of anything. I want to be a player, Frankie. I want to make a difference to the cultural life of my community." Her lip trembled, and she said, "KLEG validates me."

"I'd rather have validated parking than anything to do with this place," he snapped. Now Caroline would start in on how no one in the family had ever taken her seriously because she was a girl, and how Franklin owed it to her to let her run KLEG so she could develop self-esteem and feel good about herself. He quickly changed the subject.

"Okay, okay. But at least we have to do something about Teresa. She was in collusion with Ed and made it look like the Home Run Escort Service was part of KLEG. If that kind of disloyalty and bad judgment isn't grounds for firing someone, I don't know what is."

"How can we fire her?" Caroline said contemptuously. "We don't even know how to find her, do we? For somebody who's supposed to be so smart—"

"You couldn't find Ed, either, when I finally persuaded you to fire him. Doesn't this indicate a lack of control?"

"My management style isn't about control," said Caroline.

"Send her a letter," he said. "You have her address, don't you? How do you pay her? How can you send her a W2 at the end of the year?"

"What's that?" said Caroline defensively.

"A document that tells the employee how much you told the IRS you paid them," he said. "Everyone in the country gets one."

"I don't think Teresa does, but I'll have to ask Judy about that," said Caroline airily. "I don't micromanage. Anyway, I do know we send her checks to a P.O. box."

"It seems to me that running this place is just too much for you," said Franklin. "Vice rings! Phantom employees! Red ink! Listen, even a low-powered AM station is worth something these days. You can take your half of the money and start some other business to make you feel good about yourself. Some pottery boutique or something."

"But I *love* KLEG. Just as Mama did." She managed to imply that Franklin was a disloyal son.

"If KLEG means so much to you, why don't you buy me out? I'll sell you my half cheap, believe me." Franklin knew this would never work, but he brought it up occasionally to try to get it into Caroline's dim brain that KLEG was an asset, not just a source of emotional enrichment for her.

Caroline lived on the income from a trust their father had set up for her. Before he died, the old man had taken Franklin aside and said, "With your sister's taste in husbands, a trust fund is the only way I can keep her from being a burden to you someday." Caroline simply didn't have access to capital to buy him out. He'd have to bring her gradually to her knees, watching KLEG slowly bleed to death.

"Don't be silly," said Caroline. "We should be concentrating on making KLEG pay for itself, not talking about selling it. And if we want to be profitable, we can't fire Teresa. You keep telling me that without her we'd lose a lot of our revenue."

Franklin sighed. Caroline was right, of course. "Yes, I know. But that answering-machine stunt of hers shows poor judgment. I think we'd better at least find her and tell her so. She's clearly a loose cannon."

"All right. I'll send her a note asking her to call me." As it always did, Caroline's big-sister self-assurance returned. She gave him a patronizing smile and said, "I'm delighted you're taking an interest in the station, Frankie, but I'm afraid I've got to run. I've got a Women Managers in Media meeting."

Franklin felt vanquished again. As he left, he tried to cheer himself up by booming in a thunderous voice for the staff's benefit: "Don't let them have that Grove's *Dictionary*, Caroline. They don't need to know anything about music to play a few CDs, for Christ's sake."

Phil, who had been muttering conspiratorially with Judy, turned and glared at him. Franklin gave him a wide, wolfish smile. "Hang in there, Phil," he said.

Judy was emitting her own death-ray gaze, and he gave her a saucy wink. Let her sue him for sexual harassment. Fuck 'em if they couldn't take a joke.

As he headed for the door to the parking lot, he collided with the new woman, Alice Jordan, coming in. She presented a nice professional appearance, with her leather briefcase and neat suit, but her body language—slumped shoulders, sad little mouth—indicated defeat.

"How's it going? Sell anything yet?" he said in a belligerent voice.

"No, actually," she said.

Franklin, against his better judgment, felt a little sorry for her. After all, selling advertising on KLEG was probably about as easy as selling toxic waste. "Well, don't worry," he said. "It takes a while to polish your skills."

To his horror, Alice's eyes began to glaze over with tears. "I'm afraid—I'm afraid—" she stammered.

"Don't be afraid. What's the worst they can do?" he barked at her. "Say no, right?" If she was one of those women who wept their way through life, she might be able to pick up a few orders based on pure pity from feebleminded advertisers. But it was more likely that she'd fold and crumple and be gone in a week.

"I'm afraid the worst they can do," she said, biting her lower lip and straightening up in an apparent attempt to project bravery, "is to cancel an existing contract."

Judy piped up from the reception desk, "What? You mean you started out by losing business! Who is it?"

"Carlson's Clock Shop," said Alice in a trembly voice. "Ed hadn't been there for years, and they forgot they were on the air with us, I guess."

"That's *This Date in Music*," Judy hissed. "I produce that! Every day I find some interesting thing that happened on this date in music. It was on today's date in music that Ernest Chausson died in a bicycle accident in 1899."

"Well, forget about it, Judy," said Franklin. "We don't need it unless it's sponsored. You can use the extra time to answer the phones more expeditiously." He gestured toward a leggy yellow-ish philodendron in the corner of the reception area. "Or water these plants. I always thought *This Date in Music* was pretty hokey anyway."

Phil said angrily, "Our listeners love theme programming! We can't just cancel *This Date!* It's been running for years."

"Yeah," said Franklin. "Ever since the Chausson bicycle tragedy, no doubt."

"I trust you're planning to get a new sponsor for *This Date*," Judy said to Alice in frigid tones.

"Might not be as easy as marketing the kind of dates Ed was selling." Franklin smirked, jingling his car keys and sauntering out. Over his shoulder he said to Judy, "After you finish with the plants, you might want to clean that bathroom. It could sure use it."

"I can't believe it!" said Phil after Franklin had left. "The whole reason we do *This Date* and *Phono-Music Quiz* and *Composer's Corner* and *Today's Tone Poem* is so we have that personal touch, communicating with our listeners. Otherwise we just sound like some preprogrammed, automated, cold, impersonal music service. Without theme programming, a trained chimp could run this place. Doesn't he get it?"

Judy gave him what Alice interpreted as a warning look, as if they thought she'd snitch about this outburst to Franklin. She seized the opportunity to ingratiate herself. "I agree with you," she said. "I haven't been here very long, but I'm sure it's that warm, personal touch that makes KLEG so special. I love to learn new things myself, and I'm going to try very hard to find a sponsor for *This Date.*"

"It's important for me to have a creative outlet," whined Judy. "*This Date in Music* gave me that. It's not like I really need my master's degree to water the plants and clean toilets. I just happen to believe in classical music!"

"I'm not sure the Franklin Paynes of this world understand how some of us feel about the arts," said Alice solemnly.

Judy gave her a wary little smile.

Alice smiled back. "By the way, whatever you did to your hair, it looks really good, Judy. You'll look great on TV tonight."

CHAPTER EIGHT

That evening, members of the KLEG-AM programming staff met at Daphne Hamilton's tiny apartment to watch television coverage of Ed Costello's murder. Judy and Phil sat on the bed, pushed against the wall with a row of cushions turning it into sort of a sofa. Carl Weeb and Bob LeBaron sat on creaking wicker chairs underneath Daphne's framed black-and-white glossies of herself in various stage roles in local theater productions.

Daphne was draped in a filmy caftanlike garment, and had arranged herself on a pile of ethnic cushions on the floor, like an odalisque on her side. One hand supported her head; the other held the television remote. For the moment, the mute button was on as the local news team covered a fire in a warehouse.

Judy Livermore was giving the others an update on the phone calls she had monitored during the past week, and she had saved the best for last.

"This is the real bombshell," she said solemnly. "I knew it was important, because Ed went into the break room and closed the door. Then the button lit up, so I knew he was using the phone in there and wanted privacy. He didn't want me to overhear his side of the conversation."

The others made little noises indicating their disapproval of Ed's wanting to make a private call.

"Well?" demanded Daphne impatiently. "What did you hear?" Like many dramatic people, Daphne resented others milking anything for cheap thrills, and Judy was stretching this one out.

"He was calling Franklin Payne at his office," announced Judy.

Bob LeBaron clicked his tongue. "I'm not surprised. Haven't I always said Ed was nothing but a management spy?" He looked around with an I-told-you-so expression, but no one gave him the satisfaction of acknowledging his prescience.

"What did they talk about?" demanded Daphne.

Judy leaned over for full effect and lowered her voice to a whisper, although there was no reason to believe Caroline or Franklin had bugged Daphne's apartment. "He asked Franklin if he was interested in selling the station!"

There was a collective intake of breath. "Franklin said he'd be glad to listen to any offer!"

Phil's hands went into fists. "How disgusting," he said.

"Listen to this!" Judy's eyes were narrowed into glittery slits. "Ed asked Franklin if there would be a finder's fee if he could come up with a buyer. Franklin said, 'Absolutely,' and asked Ed if he had any leads."

"Thirty pieces of silver," said Phil Bernard, shaking his head sadly.

Judy went on. "Ed said he just might and he'd get back to Franklin. And then Franklin said in that sarcastic way of his, 'You might try selling a few ads while you're at it.'"

"Finally, proof of what we all suspected!" said Bob LeBaron. "They want to throw us into the gutter!"

"Maybe new buyers would be okay," said Daphne hopefully. "They might keep the format and put some money into the place."

Bob LeBaron tossed back his head. "Ha! No one wants an AM classical station."

Phil snapped, "I don't see why all this fuss about an FM signal. It's just like this mad rush to CDs."

There was a brief silence during which no one challenged Phil's views on new technology. Daphne glanced nervously at the screen to see if the news was now covering Ed's murder. Instead, there was some kind of chart describing how much it cost to send a kid to college.

"What about Caroline?" said Carl Weeb in his feathery little voice. "Do you think she knows?"

"Of course she does," hissed Judy. "She pretends to care about classical music and the KLEG staff, but I bet she just wants to make a quick buck off their inheritance herself."

"Oh!" Daphne was sitting up now and squealing and flapping her arms. "Here it is." She hit the mute button, and they all watched the television screen intently. A couple of men were rolling a gurney with the shrouded corpse through the KLEG parking lot.

"The victim, Ed Costello," said the announcer, "has been linked to an escort service headquartered at the classical music station. Station employees expressed shock at the slaying."

The scene shifted to a close-up of Judy, and the words "Caroline Parker, station manager" appeared along the bottom of the screen. "We were all surprised about the escort service," Judy said. "Ed was supposed to be selling ads."

"They got my name wrong!" said Judy indignantly. Now Caroline's horsey face came into view. Across her shoulders white lettering read, "Judy Livermore, station receptionist." Caroline was saying, "Poor Ed. He was devoted to classical music. We're all in shock at this terrible tragedy, especially as it comes so close to the Marjorie Klegg Payne Awards."

"They got my title wrong, too," Judy whined. "And they cut out all the stuff I said. I had a whole big thing about the station and what an asset it is to the community."

"In other news," said the blonde anchorwoman, "it looks like we'll all be paying more for home heating oil next winter."

Daphne surfed over to other channels, but there wasn't anything more about Ed's murder. She flung the remote aside and collapsed back on her cushions. "It's all so terrible," she said in her lovely contralto. "We're not even famous enough to have anyone care when something like this happens at the station!"

Bob said, "Frankly, it's probably a good thing that Ed was killed. When he was, I mean," he added hastily. "He may not have had time to line up a buyer."

Judy smiled. "I think you're right. I don't think he did. Because I overheard Franklin talking to that Alice. He said he wanted to go through all the papers on Ed's desk with her. I bet he's looking for the name of a potential buyer."

"The Paynes are probably planning to use this new woman as some kind of a fifth column," said Bob LeBaron. "We've got to be very careful what we say around her."

"Aren't you being a little paranoid?" said Daphne, rearranging her draperies. "From what I can tell, she's just a sweet housewife looking for a glamour job."

"Maybe," said Judy, clenching her jaw in a determined way. "And maybe not. She pretended to understand us today when

Franklin talked about getting rid of *This Date*. But I'm not sure I trust her. Don't worry. I'll keep an eye on her."

Phil took off his glasses and polished them on the sleeve of his sweater. His giant eyes suddenly looked tiny and weak. "I can't believe he wants us to get rid of *This Date*," he said sadly. "It's a wonderful tradition. And he was really crass and terrible about the Grove's. Caroline was just about to see the light, I just know it."

"Let's face it, all Franklin cares about is money," said Daphne with a melancholy shake of her head. "What a sad, shallow little man."

"You know what?" said Phil, replacing his glasses and surveying them all. "I wonder if Franklin didn't know about Ed's little scheme and that escort service. Today, in Caroline's office, he acted all cut up because Ed's enterprise had been closed down. He called it the station's only profit center."

Judy drew in her breath sharply. "If he wasn't profiting himself, why should he say a thing like that? God, it makes sense, doesn't it? It's just the kind of thing Franklin would do. Use KLEG for his own greedy, immoral ends! We should share our suspicions with the police.

"They asked me if I knew about the escort service. They asked to see the phone bills and acted suspicious when I said I hadn't noticed Ed had his own line into the station, but what am I anyway, some kind of a bean counter? *Light* bookkeeping, that's all my job description says."

"I bet those women who worked for Ed got more an hour than we get a week," said Carl wistfully.

"Using Ed to answer the phone was a shrewd move," said Bob. "You know, Ed always was a party guy. When we were back together at KZZ in the good old days, he used to set the clients up with this wild group of gals—"

Judy cut him off. Bob was the only one among them who'd actually been a broadcasting success before being a failure, and the others resented it. "Was it really Teresa's voice on that machine in Ed's cubicle?" she asked.

"It sure sounded like Teresa to me," said Bob.

"Wow," said Daphne. "The mysterious Teresa actually did know one of us. And it was Ed. That's very, very weird."

"I guess the cops are going to find her now," said Bob. "It should be interesting to see what she actually looks like."

"Maybe she's someone who was disfigured in some horrible way," said Daphne with a little thrill in her voice. "Like the Phantom of the Opera. And all she has left is her voice and her memories."

"Memories are all any of us may have of KLEG if that bastard Franklin Payne gets his way," muttered Bob LeBaron.

Judy raised a fist in the air. "He must be stopped! And if there's any justice, he will be. Just like Ed was."

CHAPTER NINE

Detective Lukowski didn't have any trouble finding Teresa Hoffman's address. Although she didn't have a driver's license or a phone, she was listed in the city directory. She lived downtown, in an old brick apartment building near the bus station. Back in the twenties the place had probably been pretty stylish, but now the big terra-cotta urns with juniper shrubs flanking the front step were littered with cigarette butts and beer cans, and the handsome brass-trimmed glass door led to a dimly lit lobby with peeling paint and a worn carpet.

Teresa's apartment was on the ground floor and Lukowski leaned on the bell outside her door, producing an ear-piercing, old-fashioned mechanical buzz. There was no answer, so Lukowski scribbled a note on the back of his card asking her to phone him and wedged the card between the door and the jamb. As he turned to go, he was sure he heard a klunking sound from inside the apartment, like an interior door closing. He tried the bell again, using the shave-and-a-haircut-two-bits rhythm that made people think you were a friend instead of a salesman or a cop. There was still no answer.

From the sidewalk outside the building, Lukowski looked at

Teresa Hoffman's windows. There were three of them. Two had old-fashioned window shades drawn down the whole way. The third provided a view of a kitchen. There was an old stove with a big greasy cast-iron pot on it, a sink full of dirty dishes, and a table with a faded cloth piled with a collection of odds and ends—old newspapers, a ball of string, empty mayonnaise jars, a few houseplants, a stack of folded grocery bags.

Lukowski had made a point of listening to Teresa's show the previous night. The woman had a voice full of husky sexual promise. She managed to sound as if she was recording her patter while wearing a slinky negligee and sprawling on a satin couch piled high with pillows. Teresa's apartment, however, hardly looked like a sex palace. In fact, it looked rather like his grandmother's apartment back in Chicago before his parents had put her in a nursing home.

Lukowski was more successful in finding Carmen's boyfriend. The license-plate number Alice Jordan had supplied was for a red Corvette registered to a Brad Jenkins, who lived in a modern apartment complex at the north end of the city, where suburbia began. It wasn't hard to spot the red Corvette in the parking lot. Apparently Brad was home.

A little label with "Jenkins/Davis" next to it gave him the apartment number. He pushed about five other buttons, yelled "UPS" into the intercom when the first voice said "Yes?" and was rewarded with a buzz.

A sleepy-looking dark woman in a plaid bathrobe and a pair of fuzzy socks answered his knock. A TV blared in the background. She looked about twenty, with uncombed hair and a sweet little face.

"Is Brad here?" said Lukowski, handing her a business card.

She drew her brows together and looked nervous. "He's asleep," she said. "We both work nights."

"Well, could you please wake him up?" said Lukowski. "I want to ask him a few questions. It's part of a criminal investigation."

"Who is it, Jodie?" said a male voice from inside.

"A police officer," she answered, stepping aside. Brad appeared, wearing silk boxer shorts with penguins all over them and a big T-shirt. He was about six-three, with huge biceps and calves, a neck like a tree trunk and a massive chest. He was holding a spoon and a large bowl of what appeared to be Cocoa Puffs.

"Hey, if it's about those college kids I bounced out last night, I gotta tell you, they were plenty disruptive," he said defensively.

"I'm not interested in any college kids," said Lukowski.

"They were bothering the other customers," Brad continued.

"I'm investigating the murder of Ed Costello," said Lukowski. "Can I come in and ask you a few questions?"

Brad shrugged and backed away and said, "Sure. But I don't know nothing about Ed Costello." The woman pulled her robe around her tightly and gave the sash an extra cinch.

Lukowski stepped inside. The apartment was neat and tidy, with the carefully inoffensive look of a doctor's waiting room. Besides the giant TV, there were a few matching upholstered pieces and a big framed print of a stylized mountain and water landscape of the kind sold in furniture stores as "accessories." On the oak coffee table was a row of overlapping fashion magazines, a TV remote control and a circle of milk, where the Cocoa Puffs had presumably been sitting. A kitchen was visible to the right.

The woman picked up the remote and hit the mute button,

leaving the silent image of a slatternly blonde with the words "Had Affair with Sister's Husband" across her chest. Lukowski, who had conducted plenty of interviews in homes where the TV was blaring, took the voluntary muting as a sign that these people were trying to be gracious. The three of them sat down.

"So, Jodie, are you Carmen?" he said to the woman in a friendly tone. "Is that a working name?"

She shrugged and tried to look blasé. "Kinda."

Lukowski took that as an affirmative. "I understand you think Ed Costello owed you some money," he went on. "I guess you worked for the Home Run Escort Service."

"I don't know if I wanna talk about this without an attorney," said Jodie as if by rote, picking nervously at one of her fuzzy socks. Without her makeup, and in this cozy little outfit, her long red nails looked rather grotesque.

"I'm not interested in what you and your dates did," he said. "This isn't a vice matter, it's homicide."

Brad weighed in with his legal opinion. "It's probably okay, honey."

"How much money did Ed owe you?" said Lukowski.

She shrugged. "Eight-fifty."

"Did he usually stiff the girls?"

"Ed? No. It's just that with the credit card stuff we had to wait a day or two. But then he disappeared. When we heard what happened to him, we figured someone else owed it to us. I mean *someone* has to owe it to us, right? His boss or whatever. I mean, does the credit card company keep the money?"

"His boss?"

Brad cleared his throat. "Yeah. You can't tell me that guy at the station didn't know what was going on. He must have been skimming off something. For rent."

"We have no evidence that the people at the radio station knew anything about this," said Lukowski. "But we'd like to know just how Mr. Costello's operation worked."

Jodie shrugged. "How do you think it worked? Ed answered the phone. Beeped us. Kept a percentage. We kept all the tips. Ed was a smooth guy on the phone. Made everything sound, you know, classy." She wrinkled her nose. "Not like some of the sleazebags in this business."

"How did he find you?"

"Oh, we found him," she said. "There's a bunch of us used to work for this old bitch up on Queen Anne Hill. She got greedy, so one of us asked Ed if he'd handle the business side of things."

"Who recruited Ed?"

"Her name's Lindsey. She knew him 'cause he used to put together parties for his clients at some radio station."

Lukowski nodded. "So did Ed like to party, too?"

"Ed? No way. He was too pussy-whipped. That spend-spend-spend wife of his had him by the throat. Ed was strictly a salesman. He thought up that dorky baseball name. I thought it was lame, but he said the customers would feel more comfortable if it sounded kind of all-American, you know."

Lukowski turned to Brad. "Did *you* try to collect from Ed at some point? Maybe go down to the radio station and confront him?"

Brad held up his hands in a gesture of surrender. "Hey, no way!"

"Mind telling me where you were at one o'clock last Thursday morning?"

"I was working." Brad named a rowdy Pioneer Square club where he was employed as a bouncer. He gave a big dumb grin. "I got, like witnesses and everything."

"So what are you girls going to do now that Ed's out of the picture?" said Lukowski, turning to Jodie.

"I don't know. I'm thinking of going back to school. Maybe become a dental hygienist," Jodie added without enthusiasm.

Lukowski had a hard time imagining her poring over plaster casts of teeth and memorizing facts about gum disease. "Yeah. Okay," he said skeptically. "It's probably a lot less dangerous."

Why was he even bothering? As far as Lukowski was concerned, smart, sensible hookers existed only in the movies. If he needed any more proof that Jodie had poor judgment, he had only to look at the oafish Brad.

"Dangerous?" Jodie rolled her big brown eyes and gave him a look that said, "I know how to handle myself."

"Involvement in this kind of activity may be what got Ed Costello killed," said Lukowski.

She shrugged and said, "Whatever."

"Did Ed have any enemies that you know of?"

"Ed? No. He was nice to everyone. It's too bad about what happened to him."

"Yeah it is. Listen, I want the names of the other girls. And the woman on Queen Anne you used to work for."

Jodie had a wary look in her dark eyes. "I'm not sure I can remember."

"Don't give me a hard time," Lukowski said in a slightly louder voice. "Someone in your business can't afford to mess with me, okay?"

"Okay. But you won't tell anyone I gave you their names and numbers, will you?" She went over to the phone in the kitchen and picked up paper and pen. While she was writing down names and numbers Brad said, "Think Ed's wife has Jodie's money?"

"I think you'd better not try to shake down anyone else for a debt that's the result of criminal activity," said Lukowski. "Especially when the guy you think owes it has been shot to death. You might just get yourself messed up in something you can't muscle your way out of."

Brad mulled over this advice. "Bummer."

"Gee, Brad," Lukowski said sarcastically. "Maybe you'll just have to live with the thought that a couple of guys screwed your girlfriend for free."

CHAPTER TEN

After a series of harassing phone calls to the police, implying that business had ground to a screeching halt and the station was losing a huge amount of business because the police had all of Ed's papers, Franklin finally got them to release the box.

Before sharing it with Alice, he decided to go through it himself. Locking himself in his office and asking his secretary to hold all calls, he began his search. It didn't seem very promising. There was nothing that looked remotely like a legitimate buyer.

He dismissed the leads file, shuddering for a moment at the *Asian Dolls* catalog. That would have been a humiliating addition to the KLEG client roster! Ads for diminutive, obedient wives. Or maybe Ed was using this to recruit these poor women for his stable.

Franklin began phoning the numbers he found jotted down on Post-it notes. He reached a chiropractor's clinic, a few advertising agencies, and a golf course. He told all the receptionists that he had misdialed and hung up. When he found a number with "Gary" written on it, he dialed and actually got a real person. "Hello," said Franklin, "I'm calling on behalf of the late Ed Costello."

"Never heard of him," Gary answered in a terrified voice, slamming down the phone. Franklin thought he might be a Home Run Escort Service customer who had read about Ed's murder and was lying low. This wasn't going to be easy. With a sigh, he decided he'd been crazy to think he could track down Ed's mystery buyer. Anyway, if the buyer was serious, he would contact Franklin himself, wouldn't he? But what if he called the station and talked to Caroline?

Ed had said on the voice-mail message that the prospective buyer was someone who'd once worked with him in radio. Seeing as Ed had worked at every station on the dial in his long, sagging career in radio sales, the possibilities were practically endless.

Franklin stirred around in the box and came up with one more message. This one said "Chip," and the name had dollar bills doodled next to it. This was promising.

Chip had a machine, which announced in deadpan tones: "If you are interested in educational tapes exposing the U.S. government's complicity in a conspiracy going back to a secret order of medieval Knights Templar on a small Mediterranean island, press one now. If you love freedom, are willing to lay down your life for the right to resist the forces of one-world government, and are interested in rigorous military training in a remote setting to prepare for the day of reckoning, press two now. If you want to learn how Seattle public schools are brainwashing our youth, making them into zombies in the service of world government and dupes in an international campaign against the Anglo-Saxon race, press three now. If you are interested in one of our convenient and economical Armageddon survival kits, press four now. If you have a message for Chip, press five."

Franklin was tempted to leave a message for Chip offering, as a public service, to buy him a lobotomy. Instead he hung up in disgust.

Those doodled dollar signs no doubt meant that the services Chip wanted to buy from Ed's escorts would cost a lot extra. Perhaps he'd requested the statuesque and Aryan-looking Dagmar doing something mean-spirited in a Waffen-SS uniform accessorized with heels and a whip.

Making these calls was ridiculous and beneath his dignity. Franklin suddenly realized he'd have to be out of his mind to think that a loser like Ed Costello could have come up with a legitimate buyer for KLEG. Ed was a complete scammer, and Franklin was ashamed to think he'd bought into one of Ed's cheap come-ons on the basis of that posthumous voice-mail message.

With a decisive air, Franklin threw all the Post-it notes back into the box and carried it out to his secretary. "Would you please seal this up and send it by courier over to KLEG?" he said. When he saw Winston Smith, another of the firm's attorneys, wandering into the reception area, he added in a loud voice, "Be sure to bill it to my personal account." Winston was the office snake, always looking for something to use against his partners.

"Still screwing around with the little radio station that time forgot, huh?" Winston said, with a smirk that went beautifully with his heavily starched, striped Brooks Brothers shirt and pale yellow suspenders. "Haven't you unloaded that yet?"

"I'm working on it," muttered Franklin, feigning a deeper interest in his handful of phone messages than he actually felt.

"Hope that albatross isn't interfering with your practice of law," said Winston in less than sympathetic tones.

Franklin ignored him and scurried back into his own office in an agitated state. One of the messages was from someone named Chip. His number looked like the one Franklin had just called, only to get that fruitcake voice-mail menu.

Great! First ill-mannered prostitutes show up at the office. Thank God Winston had been off playing squash during that little scene! Now Franklin supposed he'd have to prepare for Führer Chip with an assault rifle. He tore the message into little pieces and threw it in the wastebasket.

Alice spent a soul-shattering morning calling on businesses that had once advertised on KLEG. Vinyl Value Mart was a shop in the University District specializing in used LPs. The owner, a portly aging hippie with a moth-eaten-looking beard, said he'd love to be back on the air. "But it's not a good time right now," he said sadly. "My old lady needs an operation, and the house needs a new roof. Seems like everything falls apart at once."

At Barb 'n' Betsy's Beans, a gourmet coffee-bean shop in trendy Madison Park, a couple of blond women who looked like overaged sorority girls explained that the advertising budget was pinched because business just wasn't very good lately. The ladies wore matching pink-and-white striped aprons with "Barb" and "Betsy" embroidered on their chests and a lot of diamond jewelry. "Our husbands told us that this place is getting to be more than just a convenient tax write-off thing," said Barb fretfully.

Betsy piped up in a hurt voice, "Starbucks has done so well. I don't get it."

"Maybe advertising would help," suggested Alice.

"For now I think we'll just stick to the Junior League newsletter," said Barb nervously.

In a slightly defensive tone, Betsy added, "We're thinking of bringing in a line of really lovely dried flower arrangements. We met this neat gal who makes them at a women's entrepreneurs fair. They're very unique."

"When should I get back to you?" asked Alice, sure that by the time she did, the husbands would have pulled the plug on this marginal enterprise.

Her third stop was at Flexomorph, a company selling adjustable beds from a 1-800 number. They were located in grim warehouse offices in an industrial park south of the airport near the county line. Here Alice's sales call was aborted by a frowning receptionist who pointed silently to a sign on her desk: Salespeople May Call on Thursdays between 1:00 and 2:00 P.M. Apparently, around here, flexibility applied only to the beds themselves.

With reactions like this from established customers, Alice wondered how she could ever make cold calls on potential new clients. God, she thought to herself as she drove the twenty miles back to the station from Flexomorph, why didn't I listen to Mom and get a teaching certificate years ago? I could have had a steady job, summers off with Zack, and a retirement plan.

Remembering Franklin Payne's suggestion that she listen to competing AM radio stations, Alice fiddled with the car radio until she heard a nasal voice saying, "Yeah, I guess everyone here in the Northwest has to struggle with slugs. Let's go to the phones. Our guest today is the Happy Gardener, Ivan Dobbins."

"This is Chip," said the caller. "I'd like to say that we should all develop horticultural skills against the time when our food supply will be cut off by occupying forces."

"Well," the gardening expert said tentatively, "vegetable gardening *can* stretch your food budget."

"I'm talking about Armageddon here," said Chip. "If things keep going the way they are, I fully expect massive shortages and marauding bands of criminals stealing food from those with the foresight to plan ahead. We've got to be prepared to defend the perimeters of our crop-producing areas with weapons. No plowshares without swords. We all have a right to bear arms. Defend your crops, America. You know—"

The caller was cut off. "Interesting point of view," said the host sarcastically. "Seems like that's how Mr. McGregor felt about Peter Rabbit sniffing around his garden. Marge from Tacoma, you're on the air."

After interviewing Dagmar a.k.a. Lindsey, Amanda a.k.a. Trisha, Dominique a.k.a. Kim, and Candy, whose real name was Candy, Lukowski was discouraged. The women all gave him the same basic story he had heard from Carmen a.k.a. Jodie: Ed Costello had done a competent job of lining them up with out-of-town businessmen, straying husbands reluctant to cruise Aurora Avenue, yuppie scumbags who didn't want the hassle of pretending to be interested in their sexual partners' personality traits or emotional needs, and various loners who were too ashamed to reveal their specialized sexual tastes to women they might have to face later in a social situation.

Ed had run ads in the Yellow Pages and newspapers, answered the phone, reassured the customers, quoted rates accurately, sent the girls out on dates to hotel and motel rooms, bachelor parties and private homes.

As far as these women knew, no one had ever bothered Ed, and Ed hadn't bothered anyone. They couldn't recall any customer who felt aggrieved for any reason other than his own inability to get it up, usually due to too much booze.

As for the woman on Queen Anne Hill who had run the Sleek and Sassy Escort Agency, where the girls had previously worked, she had apparently retired and moved to a luxury mobile home near Palm Springs with her companion of many years, a cocktail waitress and former semiprofessional golfer, and their three miniature schnauzers, Larry, Moe and Curly.

Was there someone who felt that Ed Costello had lured a young woman into prostitution? A parent, sibling or lover? The girls all scoffed at that idea. Ed wasn't a pimp, just a business manager. He never recruited new girls. And their own families, they all maintained, had no idea what they did and wouldn't care if they did.

Lukowski reminded himself that hookers were liars by definition. Their whole way of life was based on the one big lie guys either were dumb enough to believe or were willing to overlook in a commercial transaction, which was of course that the girls enjoyed their work. But their stories seemed to ring true.

His colleagues in vice had never had dealings with Ed Costello, but said they'd ask around. They were thinking of launching another one of their halfhearted undercover operations aimed at call-out sex services, and maybe something would turn up then. Meanwhile, they were struggling along, trying to keep street prostitution and its accompanying drugs, disease and violence contained.

Lukowski's partner, MacNab, had ascertained that Mrs. Costello had no apparent motive to have her husband removed from the picture. His term life insurance policy was skimpy— about enough to bury him in style. He'd cashed in a hefty whole life policy a few years back when he was in financial straits. KLEG didn't provide its employees with life insurance. As a line of credit, Ed Costello was clearly more valuable alive than dead, at least as long as he kept answering his private line down at the radio station.

According to Mrs. Costello's confidantes—her hairdresser, personal trainer, professional shopper, nail technician, tennis coach and masseuse—she never complained about her husband or intimated there was anyone else in her life. Her tennis bracelet alibi worked out just fine. If she'd eliminated her husband, it wasn't for any easily apparent motive, and she would have had to hire the job out.

Lukowski began to think that he'd have to investigate other aspects of Ed's life more thoroughly. This was a daunting task, considering he was working about five other active cases at the moment and had two more coming to trial. He supposed he'd better ask more questions down at that creepy little radio station. Beginning, he decided, with the elusive Teresa.

CHAPTER ELEVEN

When Alice got back to KLEG, Judy said in a menacing way, "Out trying to sell, huh? Any luck?" Alice just shrugged, and Judy handed her a phone message. "This person says they want to advertise. A big schedule. Try not to discourage them."

Over at her desk Alice discovered a large box. It seemed to be the box of papers Franklin had talked about. Pushing it aside, she eagerly phoned the travel agency that had left her a message.

A pleasant-sounding young man said he was considering a saturation schedule promoting a classical music cruise. Off-season Seattle Symphony performers and members of the Seattle Opera Chorus would be on board to provide chamber music and vocal concerts. Eagerly, Alice wrote down the details.

"So tell me something about your audience," said the young man.

"Well," she began, "of course, they love classical music. And they're very loyal. A testimonial from one of our personalities goes a long way."

"Are they real old?"

"I think you'll find we have a stable, mature audience," she said nervously.

"Good. These cruises go over big with old people. In fact, we always bring a couple of coffins, just in case. How soon can we get on the air?"

"The sooner the better, I guess," said Alice. Presumably he wanted to reach customers before they dropped dead. "I can come over with a contract this afternoon. If you hang on for a minute, I'll tell you how much the kind of schedule you've described will cost."

After tapping away on her calculator, she announced that the advertising would cost fourteen hundred dollars. "That's our economy package with ads rotating in all day parts except Teresa, Queen of the Night," she explained, pleased with herself for having familiarized herself sufficiently with the rate card.

"Oh, I only want to pay if the advertising pulls," said the man pleasantly. "We'll give you a hundred bucks for every warm body you can deliver."

"But that's not how it works," said Alice, trying not to sound desperate. "Maybe you'd like a smaller schedule." She was horrified to hear herself cranking down the size of the contract, but what else could she do? God, if she didn't get these people on the air, what would Judy say? "A smaller schedule to start with," she added hastily. "I'm sure when you start getting results—"

"Results are all I care about. We'll give you a hundred bucks per inquiry. Take it or leave it."

"I'll check with my boss," she said, trying to keep her voice from quavering, "and get back to you."

"Okay," said the man cheerfully. "If it works out, maybe we can advertise again in the fall. We're doing a Mexican cruise with heart-healthy, low-sodium, high-fiber cuisine and low-stress water aerobics in the pool."

"Sounds like a lot of fun," said Alice.

As soon as she hung up and found Franklin's number, Judy's voice drifted over the side of the cubicle from the reception area. "Well?" she demanded. "Did you sign them up? I hope you got them to sponsor *This Date.*"

Tempted to shout "Back off!" Alice quickly began jabbing telephone buttons. "Sorry, I'm on another call," she said brusquely.

Franklin answered with his usual impatient tone. "Hello, Alice. What is it?"

"That box of papers has arrived," she said. "The one you said we should go through together."

"I'm afraid I'm too busy right now," he said. "Why don't you see for yourself if there's anything valuable in there?"

"All right," she said, feeling rejected. "Oh, there's another thing. I've got someone who wants to buy ads but only if they work. They want to pay us a bounty on everyone who responds."

"I think we do some stuff on a per inquiry basis with no guaranteed times. Like those ads for adjustable beds. God, it's all so pathetic. Why don't you check with Caroline? She's supposed to be in charge."

Alice was puzzled. Franklin had seemed so eager to help her, and now he sounded as if she was bothering him. Was it because he had taken a personal dislike to her? Was it something she had done? Already beaten down by rejection from the advertisers, she felt especially vulnerable right now.

She told herself to calm down and consider the source. Franklin Payne was a strange man, always frazzled and irritable and rude. Now he just sounded depressed. The whole staff apparently hated him, and his own sister didn't seem to like him much, either.

✳　　✳　　✳

As Daphne sauntered into the record library to pick up the CDs for her shift, Carl Weeb waved a sheet of creamy paper at her. "Teresa got another mash note," he said.

"Oh, really," said Daphne. "Is it smutty? If she weren't such a slut, I would feel bad that she gets more fan mail than I do."

Carl tactfully refrained from pointing out that Daphne never got any fan mail at all. "Hardly smutty," said Carl. "This guy's got it bad, but he sounds like a real gentleman."

Daphne perched on the edge of Carl's desk and read the letter:

Dear Teresa.

I've never written a fan letter before, but as a lifelong insomniac, I must tell you what an important part you play in my life. Your intelligent but playful and—dare I say it?—sexy, yes, sexy voice makes me feel I'm not alone in the long, lonely hours before the dawn.

Lately I've found myself becoming more and more fascinated by you. Although I feel I know the real essence of you, I wish I knew more about your life.

Are you unattached? You never refer to any life's companion. I too am alone, though not, I feel, because of any inherent inability to make a special place in my life for a special woman.

As a career officer in the United States Marine Corps, recently retired in my late forties (though I am considered very fit for my age), I became used to the fellowship of other men, but was never fortunate enough to meet the right girl with whom to share my life. Now, every night, your voice gives me some inkling of the kind of happiness that has eluded me.

Would it be presumptuous of me to ask you a little about yourself? What do you look like? What do you like to do when you aren't on the air? What are your hopes and dreams? What books do you love? Are you fond of animals?

If this desire to know you better seems impertinent, please accept my apologies and ignore this letter. But be assured, Teresa, that my feelings of admiration for you are sincere and deeply felt. Count me as one of the most loyal subjects of the Queen of the Night.

With all good wishes,

Stanton P. Edgecombe, USMC Ret.

"Oh, isn't that sweet?" said Daphne.

"Yeah, there's something kinda quaint about him," said Carl. "I think he deserves a nice reply." He scrabbled in his desk drawer. "I can't find my Teresa pen. Oh. Here it is." He produced a fountain pen and unscrewed the cap thoughtfully.

Carl's job description included answering all listener mail, most of which asked about musical selections people had heard on the station, or complained about programming choices or pronunciation errors by the announcers. Some of it, however, consisted of fan mail for Teresa. Carl always hand-wrote the replies in florid penmanship with purple ink.

"Be nice to him," said Daphne. "Don't be a rotten little tease."

Carl giggled and began to write:

Dear Stanton,

Thank you for your kind letter. I really was very touched. I would be glad to let you know a little about me. It's charming that you care enough to ask. I am five-seven, with thick

black hair to my shoulders and almond-shaped gray eyes.
Many people say my mouth is my best feature.

Daphne was looking over Carl's shoulder as he laboriously
formed the fat, loopy letters. "She sounds conceited," she said.

"Oh. Okay." Carl added the words, "That's what they say, but
I don't see it myself."

He looked up at Daphne. "Do you think she likes animals?"

"Beats me. I guess I can imagine her having a cheetah on a
leash or something."

"Maybe a dovecote," said Carl. "Or some small dog with silky
fur. I think a cheetah might scare him."

Franklin was sitting in a restaurant waiting with all the sus-
pense he might have felt if he were meeting a blind date. He
checked his watch every few minutes and wondered if he'd been
stood up, smoothed his hair down, touched the knot of his tie,
chewed nervously on breadsticks, brushed the resulting crumbs
off the tablecloth, thought about ordering a glass of wine, decided against it, checked his watch again.

Two days ago he'd received a phone call from a lawyer he'd
never heard of, named Ron Ott. Ott said he represented Ed
Costello's mystery buyer. "My client is very interested in your
discretion," the guy had said dramatically. "He asks that you
don't discuss this meeting with anyone, in or out of your orga-
nization."

"No problem," said Franklin. "Can you tell me a little more
about him?"

"Not over the phone," Ott said in a stage whisper. "My client
is very concerned about security."

"Fine," said Franklin, who thought this all sounded a little pompous. "Where would you like to meet?"

"We'll call you the day of the meeting with the place."

"Okay," said Franklin, wondering just why the buyer was so shy. Nobody in Seattle, with the possible exception of Bill Gates, was so famous that they needed to sneak around like this.

The next day, Ott called back and suggested a restaurant well off the beaten track in West Seattle. Franklin had been immediately put off by the sign on the door: No Shirt, No Shoes, No Service. Inside, he was confronted with warped fake wood paneling, grubby red-and-white checked tablecloths, and a yeasty food smell that brought back his old junior high school cafeteria.

A repulsive oil painting of a gondola plying a lurid canal, a garland of plastic garlic next to the cash register, and dusty Chianti bottles with dripping candles on the tables indicated the cuisine was supposed to be Italian.

Franklin was the only customer in the place, but a haze of cigarette smoke and the sound of a blaring TV came from a dark doorway leading to what a carved wood and gilt sign indicated was the Grand Canal Room. This dump was clearly in the booze business, and the restaurant existed only to comply with state laws that forbade selling distilled beverages without also selling food. He sighed and sat down at a corner table.

A narrow-faced man of about fifty arrived, looking decidedly pathetic. Franklin took in his bad haircut made worse by some kind of greasy hair oil, his cheap suit, his plastic briefcase. He introduced himself as Ron Ott and sat down across from Franklin.

Franklin reflected that if he'd had decent taste, Mr. Ott could have bought a better haircut, suit and briefcase with the money he'd spent on the large diamond pinkie ring he wore.

"My client's running a little late," he said. "He's a busy guy."

"I see," said Franklin. "Who is he? Ed mentioned he'd worked with him in the past."

Ron Ott leaned over conspiratorially, in spite of the fact that there were no customers or staff in sight. "His name," he hissed, "is Charles W. Gilmore." He leaned back, as if this should have some effect. "Not many people know he started out as a radio engineer at KZZ."

Franklin looked blank, and Ott said, "You've heard of Mr. Gilmore, I presume?"

"The name sounds vaguely familiar," lied Franklin. Maybe he was some kind of radio preacher. Franklin hoped so. A guy like that would probably have access to a lot of money.

A bored-looking waitress emerged from the Grand Canal Room and offered them plastic menus dappled with crusty tomato-sauce spatters. Franklin glanced over the uninspired selection of allegedly Italian dishes and resisted the urge to ask if Chef Boyardee was working today, in which case he'd like the SpaghettiOs.

Ron Ott looked hurt that Franklin had never heard of Charles Gilmore. "He was involved in an important trial last year. Groundbreaking constitutional issues. I was pleased to represent him."

"I see," said Franklin, not seeing at all. He ordered a bowl of minestrone and a Caesar salad.

"I believe in freedom of speech for everyone, not just for people I agree with," explained Ott carefully, as if retailing a concept new to Franklin. "I will defend to the death any American's right to say things that I myself, personally speaking—"

Just then a short, chubby middle-aged man with a red face

and a gray crew cut that made his round head look like a hedge-hog walked into the restaurant. He was dressed in combat boots and complete camouflage gear. He approached the table.

"Here he is now," said Mr. Ott, introducing the two men with a flourish. "Franklin Payne. Charles Gilmore."

"Call me Chip," said Mr. Gilmore, in the voice Franklin recognized from the loony recorded message about one-world government and threats to the Anglo-Saxon way of life.

Gilmore leaned over the table to shake hands, and dog tags clanked against the Chianti bottle candleholder. Franklin waved a greeting rather than shake Chip Gilmore's hand, but Gilmore didn't seem to notice the insult. Scanning the restaurant with hooded eyes, he selected a chair with its back to the wall. He sat down heavily and said to Franklin, "Ed said you were a straight-up guy. Before we talk about KLEG, I'd like to say I think there may be a government cover-up going on in the matter of Ed Costello's death. There are elements of society who will do what-ever it takes to throttle the battle cries of freedom. In fact, do you know your own secretary received a message from me? I assume she destroyed it before you got it, as you didn't return the call."

"I'll look into it," said Franklin.

"That's why I use Ron here as kind of a front man," Gilmore said, narrowing his eyes. "No need to let the enemy know what I'm up to. I'd like to get on the air and tell the world a few home truths about this country and what kind of siege we're under here, before the enemy catches on."

Franklin nodded and said, "I see." He wondered if this lunkhead actually had any money. If he did, Franklin wanted it all up front. A nice clean deal.

"They tried to stop me before," said Gilmore through clenched teeth. "They threw me off the public airwaves."

Now Franklin remembered the case. A local cable outlet had decided it didn't want to run rantings from Chip Gilmore on its community access channel. Apparently he had been trying to solicit contributions and was also hawking his cranky audiotapes on the air. Some of Gilmore's goons had threatened station personnel, and the company got a restraining order keeping them away.

"We're appealing," said Ott, looking up from the menu with a statesmanlike air that didn't quite jibe with the powerful drugstore cologne he wore.

This was promising. Presumably Ott was collecting legal fees. There must be some money around. Maybe old Chip got it from robbing banks. But Franklin reflected sadly that even if Gilmore could come up with the money to buy KLEG, he'd have a hard time selling Caroline on the idea of turning Mom's Music Box over to neo-Nazis.

"Before we go any further," said Franklin, "I think you should know I figure the station's worth at least a million dollars." Franklin had just made up this figure to discourage them. These people didn't look like they could come up with the scratch to buy a used weed whacker at a yard sale.

Chip just nodded. Franklin went on, "And I'm not interested in any terms. I want strictly a cash deal. Can you line up the financing or not?"

Ott and Gilmore exchanged glances, and Gilmore said, "I don't want to tell you too much. It wouldn't be safe. I'd just like to say that Ed Costello was working on that. It's one more reason I think there may have been involvement from the enemy in his murder. Did you know the United Nations maintains a hit squad of elite killers? Gurkhas and stuff."

"Are you saying that Ed Costello was working on the financing?" said Franklin, deciding not to touch the Gurkhas as a topic of discussion and to leave as soon as possible. He hailed the wait-ress and canceled the soup and salad. "I'm feeling nauseous," he explained. Neither of his companions expressed any sympathy.

"Ed had come into some important knowledge which would have made it all possible," said Chip Gilmore dramatically. "There's some money owed to me from my past, and Ed was going to help me collect."

"Someone owed you a million bucks?" said Franklin. These people were complete losers. He glanced at his watch. "Listen, I don't think there's much point—"

"I can't tell you more now," said Gilmore tersely.

"I'll be pursuing this funding source myself," said Ott.

"Discreetly, of course," said Gilmore. "One man has already given up his life for this." Could he be referring to Ed?

Ott nodded but seemed willing to take his chances with the elite Gurkha units from the UN. "Yeah, well, it would be help-ful if we could go over Mr. Costello's papers and see if there's any clue to how his own researches were proceeding."

"Just what the hell are you guys talking about?" said Franklin. He pointed to Gilmore. "Who owes him a million bucks?"

The lawyer cleared his throat. "Sorry, but that's confidential. That information could be used to discredit Mr. Gilmore's movement," said Ott solemnly.

"By people who just don't get it," added Gilmore.

Franklin felt that Gilmore could discredit his movement all by himself without any help from anyone else. "Come up with a million dollars in cash and we'll talk," said Franklin pleasantly.

"What about access to Mr. Costello's papers?" Ott began. "That would make it easier for me to pursue—"

"The police have all that," lied Franklin. There was no way he was going to have any further dealings with these two.

Gilmore sucked his teeth. "That's bad," he said. "Real bad. That must be how they found me." He leaned over to Franklin. "The cops called and asked me if Ed had any enemies. I played dumb."

Tempted to suggest that in playing dumb Gilmore was hardly playing against type, Franklin said, "I'm curious. Was Ed involved in your, er, movement in any way?" Had KLEG been harboring a Nazi nutcase as well as a pimp?

"No," said Gilmore. "Ed wasn't ideologically motivated, but he was open to my ideas. He was a businessman. He was going to help me put together this deal to buy the station. For a finder's fee." Gilmore looked a little sentimental. "He was always like that. Way back twenty years ago when we worked at KZZ, he was always setting people up one way or another. A real middleman."

"Yeah, yeah," said Franklin. "Poor old Ed. Look, this isn't getting us anywhere, and I have a meeting I just remembered."

"We'll be in touch," said Ott, as Franklin scraped back his chair and hustled out of the restaurant.

As he got into his car, Franklin noticed two undernourished young men leaning on an old Pontiac in the parking lot. They had crew cuts and ferrety, hardscrabble faces, partially obscured by sunglasses, and they wore, like Gilmore himself, camouflage gear and combat boots. Their arms were folded belligerently across caved-in chests. Presumably they were there to make sure Gurkhas didn't storm the restaurant and slit the throat of their leader. Avoiding eye contact with these wraithlike figures, Franklin got behind the wheel of his Mercedes and sped away as fast as he could.

CHAPTER TWELVE

Lukowski went over to Teresa Hoffman's apartment determined
to speak to her. She hadn't called him, which, he felt, was pretty
nervy. If he couldn't get to her himself, he'd ask the patrol guys
to flush her out.

When he got to the apartment house, however, he was startled to see a coroner's van parked out front. He arrived in the
lobby just in time to see two guys pushing a gurney through
Teresa Hoffman's door. On the gurney was a human shape completely covered by a large sheet.

Lukowski flashed his badge and said, "What's happened?"

The attendant shrugged. "Who knows? Looks like she's been
dead about a week."

"You know who she is?"

The attendant checked a clipboard. "The apartment house
manager just left. She was pretty shook up. She identified her as
Teresa Hoffman."

Caroline didn't seem to be in her office. Alice decided to go
look for her in order to ask about the cruise organizer's request
for results-only payment.

She wandered into the record library, only to find Daphne and Carl looking up at her inquiringly. Carl immediately let his head drop back down and continued writing something.

"Oh. Hi," Alice said. "I was just looking for Caroline."

"Good luck," said Daphne. "She never makes more than a cameo appearance around here."

Carl gave a small, sly smile and kept on writing laboriously, like a child learning penmanship.

"It is a little difficult to know who's in charge around here," said Alice, pleased that Daphne had offered a small opening.

"No one's in charge," said Daphne. "But that's okay. We all know what we're supposed to be doing. Franklin and Caroline just get in the way."

Great, thought Alice. They may know what they're doing, but I don't. "So Ed pretty much supervised himself?"

"We never quite knew what he was up to, to be honest," said Daphne with a puzzled frown.

From the speaker mounted high up on the wall in the record library, Phil's reedy but sincere voice held forth. "I just had a call from some woman complaining about the sound quality on this classic LP of Schubert's 'Death and the Maiden,' with the Busch Quartet. Well, here at KLEG we're more interested in preserving legendary performances of the past, rich in a musical tradition. We're not going to throw anything off our playlist simply because it happens to have been recorded in an age that embraced musical rather than technological values. I've said it before and I'll say it again: this is the only performance of this piece worth listening to. To anyone who really cares about music, some tinny CD run off by some slick but soulless pickup quartet will never compare with the performances available on lush vinyl by an ensemble steeped in the tradition from which this music sprang.

I'm afraid I'm getting more than just a little steamed about listeners calling up and complaining about small technicalities."

In an angry tone, Phil continued, "Let me put it to you this way, and maybe some of you will get it. It's kind of like being on the Olympic Peninsula on a cloudy day such as we have here in the Northwest. You can't see every little detail of the awe-inspiring mountains, but you can sense them looming over you, and somehow they're all the more majestic shrouded in a veil of mist. Others may compromise, but here at KLEG we're holding the line. If it's musical wallpaper you want, go ahead, be my guest. Listen to that other classical station."

"Jesus," muttered Carl. "Why doesn't he just tell them KING-FM's dial position?"

Phil's voice was becoming more agitated and higher-pitched. "As long as yours truly, Phil Bernard, is on the job, we'll never change. Because Seattle deserves a world-class radio station—and we're it." Phil gasped for air, and an alarming klunking sound came from the speaker. Alice wondered if Phil, overwrought, had collapsed onto the microphone.

"He's lost it again big-time," said Daphne, clicking her tongue, "and now we've got dead air."

Phil's voice finally returned, suddenly chirpier. "Gee, I guess I was up on my high horse again, folks. Now, just to let you know we're open to new ideas, let's listen to Bach and the MOOG synthesizer. It's *Sheep May Safely Graze* from *Switched-On Bach*, Johann Sebastian at his most psychedelic."

"That's trendy," said Carl sarcastically. "How about a segue to *Night on Disco Mountain*?"

Thundering tones blasted into the room, followed by a frowning Phil, in person, carrying a coffee cup with a picture of

Beethoven on it in one hand and a tattered LP jacket in the other.

Daphne and Carl gave him baleful looks. Looking angry but defensive, he said, "Okay. Maybe I overdid it a little. At least that weasel Ed wasn't around to hear it."

"When you get upset like that," said Daphne, tilting her head to one side pensively, "you work the mike pretty close and your p's start popping."

"I salvaged the situation by pandering once again to the lowest common denominator and playing that youth-oriented thing," said Phil. He flung the Schubert LP at Carl. "This needs a good wash. None of it would have happened if someone hadn't gotten crud all over this, causing a lot of clicking. It looks like peanut butter. Have you been using the records as sandwich platters?"

"No, but I think Bob LeBaron has been eating in the booth again," said Carl. "There were a bunch of burrito wrappers in there after his last shift." Carl rose and left with the record and a bottle of Joy dishwashing liquid.

Alice glanced down at the letter Carl had been writing, managing to read the last line, which read, "Love, Teresa."

Daphne followed her eyes. "Carl answers her mail," she explained. She leaned over and said confidentially, "Poor Carl. He's auditioned a million times to be an announcer, but Phil always shoots him down. Answering Teresa's mail is as close as he'll ever get to stardom."

"You'll find that in this business everyone wants to be an announcer eventually," said Phil to Alice. "Many are called; few are chosen." He refilled his coffee cup from a thermos on his desk.

"How nice for both of you, then," said Alice pleasantly.

"Alice is looking for Caroline," explained Daphne.

"Really?" said Phil. "Why?"

"Oh, I just had a question about an advertiser."

"Well, don't expect us to help you," Phil replied. Alice hadn't had any intention of asking for anything from the querulous old man. "The only way for broadcasting to work properly," he went on, "is for the sales side of the house and the artistic side to be completely separate. Too bad Ed Costello didn't understand that."

He checked his watch and went back down the hall toward the broadcast booth.

"Phil doesn't mean to sound ungracious," said Daphne. "It's just that Ed was trying to get him fired."

"Oh, really?"

Daphne nodded. "Ed kept taping Phil's little on-air outbursts and playing them for Caroline. He said we could jack up the ratings and get more business if we got a new program director in here. He said Phil made a point of insulting what little audience we had left."

"Do you think Caroline took Ed's concerns seriously?"

Daphne shrugged. "Who knows? Phil's been here forever. Caroline's mother hired him back when hi-fi was cutting edge. KLEG is his life." She rolled her eyes as if to indicate that she had more going for her.

Alice went out past the break room. She glanced inside and saw Carl standing at the sink, scrubbing the Schubert LP with a long-handled dishwashing brush and rinsing it off under the faucet. Judy sat nearby with her back to the door, eating a depressing lunch that looked like raw carrot and rutabaga. "I think Caroline's in love again," she was saying between audible crunches. "I heard her making a lunch date with some guy who sounded like a gigolo. And I heard Alice trying to suck up to Franklin and give away ads to some travel agent."

"Maybe it would be more efficient if you just taped everyone's phone calls and circulated the cassette," said Carl in his soft little voice. Alice couldn't tell if he was kidding or not.

"I've always been attracted to older women," said Jeffrey Fleming, swirling his remaining Chardonnay, putting the glass to his lips and staring boldly at Caroline over the rim.

Caroline noticed with irritation that the impossibly young waiter, who was removing the dessert plates, seemed to be smirking at this. How dare he? Men who appreciated older women were invariably sensitive, sophisticated people who knew a lot about life, and more than a few of them had appreciated her over the years.

She smiled at Jeffrey and fingered the stainless-steel pendant that hung between her breasts from what appeared to be a bicycle chain. She felt herself blushing a little and hoped he didn't think she was having a hot flash.

He returned her smile. "How do you feel about younger men?" he went on in a husky whisper. He ran a hand through his wavy auburn hair. Jeffrey Fleming was probably ten years her junior. Except for a slightly worn-out, gaunt look, which she found attractive, attributing it as she did to his artistic temperament, he was pretty well preserved.

"I don't think age should be a barrier to—anything, really," she said, waving her hand.

He nodded. "Absolutely. Youth is a state of mind. People like us, who have lively cultural interests, why, we can go on forever."

She put her elbows on the table and set her chin girlishly on her hands in an Audrey Hepburn–like pose meant to indicate that he had her complete attention. "Speaking of which, Jeffrey, I want you to tell me all about your upcoming show." Fleming was a photographer specializing in haunting portraits of the emotionally disturbed and bleak landscapes of desert trailer parks.

"Well," he said, "there's no point in describing work verbally that should speak for itself visually. My studio's just around the corner. Why don't you come and take a look?"

"Oh, I'd be delighted. If it isn't an imposition or anything—"

"Not at all. I'd love to get your reaction. And, Caroline, to be honest, I chose this restaurant because it was just around the corner." His voice took on a new intimacy. "I was hoping to lure you up to my studio after lunch."

He reached for the check, but she stopped him, letting the tips of her fingers rest on the back of his hand for a second. "Let me get this," she said. "I'll put it on the KLEG credit card. This is business, since I've been thinking we should interview you on the station before your show. I really want us to cover the visual arts more thoroughly."

"Oh, all right," he said, settling back in his chair. "But the next time's on me. I insist."

Caroline fished in her purse for her credit card and reading glasses. She'd been dying to see his studio, and she was thrilled that he respected her artistic judgment. She also felt another kind of thrill at the prospect of the two of them alone together. Their relationship had become increasingly friendly over the half dozen lunches they'd had since meeting at the Cross-Cultural Multimedia Conference of the Visual Arts sponsored by the Majorie Klegg Payne Foundation.

"Speaking of KLEG," he said, clearing his throat, as Caroline, glasses on the end of her nose, filled in the tip amount, "I haven't seen you since poor Ed Costello died. I read all about it in the papers, and I thought of calling you and offering you some kind of sympathy. What a terrible thing!"

"It's horrible and mystifying," said Caroline. "I can't imagine who would do such a thing."

Jeffrey Fleming examined the slightly frayed cuff of his tweed jacket and said, "Ed never happened to tell you anything about me, did he?"

"Why, no," said Caroline, looking up at him with genuine surprise. "I didn't even know you knew him."

He shrugged. "You know what a small town this is in some ways. Years ago, when I was doing a lot of commercial work, I worked with an ad agency and Ed used to call on us. Last time you and I had lunch and I picked you up at KLEG, I ran into him in the parking lot. I hadn't thought about him in years. I just wondered if he'd mentioned anything about, well, you know, my past."

"No, not at all." Caroline frowned, scratched out the tip amount and redid it. That waiter had been entirely too smirky. Ten percent was enough. Bending over the tab, she didn't notice the beatific look of relief on Jeffrey Fleming's usually haggard face.

CHAPTER THIRTEEN

After learning that Judy was listening in on her calls, Alice felt diffident about making pitches on the phone. Judy would just be waiting for her to screw up. Instead, she decided to spend the afternoon making more cold calls in person. She'd managed to come up with a list of previous advertisers, augmented by a few names and addresses she found in the box of Ed's papers.

Her first stop was a dimly lit astrological bookstore in Belltown. She stepped over a couple of malt liquor cans and pushed hard at the sticking door. Inside, the little shop smelled of mildew and mothballs. A prim-looking older woman, her shiny silver hair in a pageboy held back by a black velvet headband, sat behind the counter. She was surrounded by three obese and comatose cats. The woman gave Alice an unwelcoming glance and looked back down at some knitting.

Suddenly feeling rather shy, Alice feigned interest in the merchandise—books on astrology, New Age tracts, tarot cards, a glass case full of crystals and cheap zodiac medallions.

Finally she approached the counter and said, "I'm from KLEG Radio. I believe Ed Costello called on you before."

"I've paid you something on account," said the woman in a

sharp, cultivated, fluty voice. "I'll get you the rest as soon as I can."

"Oh," said Alice, flustered. "I didn't realize there was some sort of problem."

"Problem! There certainly was a problem. I made it very clear to Mr. Costello that he was not to run those ads when Saturn was retrograde. No wonder they didn't bring in one single customer! I'm afraid I'll just have to pay you as money comes in."

"Perhaps if you tried again," began Alice. "When the stars were more—"

"Mercury is ruler of messages and communications," said the woman as if speaking to an idiot child. "Mercury won't be in the right place for me to advertise for another decade. There was just a small window of opportunity, but it's gone now, thanks to your Mr. Costello."

Apologizing, Alice backed out of the store and once again found herself blinking back tears of frustration. Tomorrow, she vowed, she'd tell Judy she was out making more cold calls and then she'd go take typing tests at temporary agencies instead.

Her next stop, she felt sure, must be a mistake. All she'd had to go on was a name and address—Rosa Delgado, Delgado Enterprises—and a suite number in a downtown high-rise. This was a far cry from the shabby, pathetic businesses she'd been visiting up to now—enterprises surrounded by an aura of dashed hopes and inevitable failure.

These top-floor offices, however, were elegant. Alice took in the vast waiting area, the pleasant-looking receptionist, the framed architectural drawings on the walls.

Alice was grateful that the receptionist was on the phone. She was able to leaf through some glossy brochures on the coffee table and discover just what this company did. Apparently, Delgado Enterprises sold condominiums. "Olympic Acres—Gracious Retirement Living in a Setting of Stunning Natural Beauty," "Lake Vista Estates—A Weekend Retreat for Year-Round Pleasure," read the captions above pictures of attractive fiftyish people fishing in bright blue waters and thirtyish yuppies drinking wine on balconies overlooking snowcapped peaks.

The atmosphere was a little too upscale for Alice to make her usual pitch leaning on the counter next to the cash register. Maybe she'd better ask for an appointment with Rosa Delgado instead.

When the receptionist got off the phone Alice approached the desk. She cleared her throat and said, "I wonder if I could make an appointment with Rosa Delgado. I should have called, but—" Now she felt awkward. How ridiculous to show up in person to make an appointment. "You see, I'm from KLEG Radio. I've just taken over from Ed Costello."

Just then a short woman in her mid-forties with heavy but artful makeup and a fabulous caramel-colored wool bouclé suit came into the reception area. The receptionist sat up a little straighter in her chair.

The woman gave Alice an appraising look. She had almond-shaped eyes behind tinted glasses, golden skin, a pile of lacquered black hair arranged on top of her head in what Alice assumed was an attempt to add a few inches.

"Ed Costello?" she said. "What about him?" She had a slight accent and a hard edge to her voice.

"I've taken over for him," said Alice. "At KLEG Radio. He was calling on you for radio advertising. I wanted to touch base with Rosa Delgado."

The woman didn't say anything, so Alice gestured toward the

brochures. "I guess you know, we have a lot of older listeners. Perfect for retirement homes."

"I'm Rosa Delgado," the tiny woman said brusquely. "Come on in. We'll talk." She flung a file folder at the receptionist and strutted into her office on three-inch heels, Alice in tow.

Rosa Delgado's office was a huge beige affair with a massive walnut desk. She got behind it, looking even tinier, and pointed to a guest chair. "So what do you want?" she said.

"Oh. I want you to buy some advertising," Alice said. "I guess Ed had already talked to you."

Rosa nodded and looked attentive. She folded her small, well-manicured hands on the desk in front of her. They were bristling with diamonds in elaborate settings.

Alice began, "To tell you the truth, I don't know much about your business. I found your name and number on Ed's desk when I took over."

"What happened to him?" demanded Rosa.

"He, um, died. It was very tragic. It was in all the papers."

"I only read the business section," said Rosa. "I don't care about all that other stuff. Too depressing."

"Tell me a little bit about your advertising needs," said Alice tentatively. "You're selling condominiums. Are they all retirement homes?"

"And time shares," said Rosa. "We have three major developments around the state. We need to get some people out to look at the units. After that, we can sell them. All we need is leads. We already advertise on radio. Why should I include your station in my budget?"

"Um, well, we have mature listeners. It's a classical station, you know. So they are more likely to be upper income." Alice had never gotten this far before. Suddenly she panicked, realizing that at some point she'd have to come out and ask this woman to buy. She rather dreaded that moment. The close, she knew they called it.

"How long have you been doing this?" said Rosa.

"About a week," said Alice, blushing.

"Sold anything yet?" snapped Rosa.

"Well, actually, I'm working on a few things—"

"Okay." Rosa, who had a stern little face with slightly flaring nostrils, suddenly broke into a friendly smile. She had beautiful teeth. "I'll be your first customer."

"Maybe Ed had already convinced you," said Alice with a self-deprecating little laugh.

"Stop it!" said Rosa, her smile vanishing. "Never put yourself down. You got a contract?"

"Oh. Yes. I do." Alice began scrabbling through her briefcase. "How much do you think you'd like to spend?"

"Take control of the sale!" said Rosa. "You tell me what I need to spend to make an impact!"

"Well," said Alice. "A big ticket item like a home, you only need to sell one to justify a very heavy schedule." She smiled, rather pleased with herself for having thought of this.

Before she knew what had happened, Alice found herself filling out a contract for Rosa Delgado to sign.

"Come back next week. I'll have a tape of the ad. It's being produced now," said her new client, signing so vigorously it seemed she might tear right through to the bottom carbon.

"Thank you very much," said Alice.

"Now tell me I won't regret this," said Rosa sternly, flinging down the pen and pushing the contract back at her. "You got to keep telling the buyer they did the smart thing."

"Oh, you won't regret this," said Alice. "I really think KLEG is a good place for you to advertise."

"Better. Did you know Ed?"

"Ed Costello? Why, no."

"Ha! Good thing he didn't train you," said Rosa. "He wasn't a very good salesman. Kind of sleazy. But you have an honest face. Even though you look scared." She leaned over confidentially. "You know what? I came to this country twenty years ago with nothing. Nothing. Now I own these developments and about ten apartment buildings around town. But I was scared at first." Rosa reached over and patted Alice's hand, jewels flashing. "You do this awhile. If you can stop looking scared and keep looking honest, maybe you can work for me. Sell some of these condominiums to empty nesters. Come back and see me later. We'll talk again." She handed over a business card. "Nice doing business with you, Alice."

Back in his office, Lukowski began to prepare a request for Teresa Hoffman's death certificate when MacNab bustled up to his desk with a piece of paper flapping.

"Something kinda interesting came up when we ran that list of Ed Costello's phone numbers and contacts through the computer," MacNab said. "Charles a.k.a. Chip Gilmore. The feds are investigating him. The guy appears to have been selling automatic weapons out of the back of his car. He's also been charged with assault a couple of times. The last time was some kind of pushing-and-shoving match outside a cable TV station.

"I talked to one of the guys who busted him for the assault thing," MacNab continued. "Apparently this character believes the UN is taking over America and the federal government is helping out by putting mind-control drugs in the glue on postage stamps. Runs some kind of weekend warrior platoon that hangs out at gun shows."

"Let's call Mrs. Costello and ask her if her husband was involved with these folks," said Lukowski. "Not that she was exactly up to speed on his activities."

He reached for the phone and learned there were two voicemail messages. The first one was from Judy Livermore, the receptionist at KLEG. "I think you should know," she said breathlessly, "that we have reason to believe Franklin Payne may know more than he lets on about Ed Costello and his criminal activities. Maybe we can arrange a meeting to discuss this further."

Lukowski sighed. He thought it pretty unlikely that Franklin Payne, a partner in a prominent law firm and somebody with family money too, would be fooling around with the Home Run Escort Service.

The second message, however, got his attention. It was the familiar sultry voice of Teresa, Queen of the Night. "I found the card you stuck in my door," she said. "Sorry I didn't call sooner. From what I've read in the papers, I guess you want to know about Ed Costello. I'm afraid I can't tell you much. I never met him. He got me to make a tape recording for an escort service, but he assured me it was just a gag—some kind of a joke he was playing on someone. He wrote me a note at my post office box with the script, and I mailed him a cassette. I'd hate it if anyone thought I had anything to do with his escort service. I thought he was just someone who worked at KLEG. Anyway, that's all I know. Good-bye."

"That's weird," Lukowski said to MacNab. "I just got a voicemail message from Teresa."

"Oh, good," said MacNab.

"Yeah, but she phoned this afternoon. At which time the

Teresa Hoffman who lives near the bus station was supposed to have been dead at least a week."

"So? She must have been the wrong Teresa Hoffman." Mac-Nab shrugged. "It's not that uncommon a name."

"Maybe not. But the Queen of the Night said she found my card in her door," said Lukowski. "And I only left one card in one Teresa's doorjamb."

CHAPTER FOURTEEN

Flushed with triumph, Alice returned to the office and casually dropped the Delgado contract on Judy's desk for processing. "I see you sold something," Judy said grudgingly.

"That's right. I pick up the tape next week," said Alice. She looked into Caroline's office, eager to report her first sale, but Caroline was gone. Over at her own desk, she dug into the box of Ed Costello's papers. Maybe there was another hot prospect in there. She'd leave no stone unturned.

"Chip" looked promising. There were dollar signs next to his name. But when she dialed the number, Alice was horrified yet intrigued to hear a recorded menu of extremist options. Apparently Chip was some kind of right-wing wacko, peddling paranoid tapes. She certainly couldn't imagine him selling that stuff on KLEG. Or maybe she could.

By the time she got to "If you have a message for Chip, press five," she recognized the voice. This was the same Chip she'd heard ranting on about vegetable gardens and guns on another radio station.

She pressed five. Maybe Chip had some other business. When she read about some of these paranoid survivalist types in the media, they often seemed to own small businesses in grungy strip malls. Maybe Chip was a tax preparer or ran a coin shop or something. If Ed hadn't left those dollar signs next to his name, she probably would have hung up.

After the beep she said in a tentative voice: "This is Alice Jordan at Classic KLEG. I found your number among the papers on Ed Costello's desk. I've taken over for him in sales. If you need an advertising schedule for a product or retail business, give me a call." She left the number.

Digging around in the box some more, like somebody pulling out a winning door prize entry, she came up with a business card for Madame Letitia's Tattoo and Body-Piercing Emporium. That hardly seemed like an appropriate advertiser for KLEG's elderly listeners, but if she could leave a message for the certifiable Chip, she could certainly call on a business engaged in voluntary mutilation. As the phone rang, Alice realized that perhaps this peculiar job was good for her. She was developing some nerve.

Madame Letitia, it transpired, was eager to advertise on the Queen of the Night's show. "Teresa is happening," she said solemnly. Alice eagerly made preparations to visit Letitia with a contract immediately.

That evening, while she and Zack ate a dinner of baked beans with sliced hot dogs, she told him about her day. "I'm so encouraged," she said. "I actually sold two schedules. Maybe this will be all right. And I even met someone who told me that after I had more experience I could apply for a job selling condominiums."

"Cool," said Zack. "Does this mean I can get a new deck for my skateboard?"

"Please stop asking for things," said Alice firmly. "How did you get to be so materialistic?"

"Not from Dad. He gave away all our money."

Alice didn't want to talk about Ken and his spectacular midlife crisis. "Listen, Zack, one of the advertisers I signed up today was a tattoo and body-piercing parlor."

"Cool," said Zack.

"The reason I brought it up is I don't want you to do anything crazy and get anything pierced or tattooed. That place was pretty scary."

"Really?"

"I heard a girl screaming when I got there," she said. "And the whole place smelled like bacon cooking. Know why?"

"No."

"They were *branding* her," said Alice, shuddering. "With a poker or something. I almost threw up. Apparently this is the latest thing. And the owner had pierced eyebrows, lips and nostrils. Not to mention a big snake tattooed all around her arm. The first thing I thought of was how awful her parents must feel."

"Oh, Mom, chill," said Zack. "I'd never do that. Unless I was like in a band or something. Anyway, you have to be eighteen or have your parents sign." After a pause he added, "I guess it's like you said before. You're getting to meet some interesting people."

"Yes, you're right," she said. Actually, Madame Letitia had been rather fascinating, and fun to talk to once you got past her disfigurements. Alice had also gotten a cheap thrill listening to Chip's recorded messages and observing the tarty escorts rampaging in Franklin's office. These characters were more like subjects for tabloid TV than anyone she'd met at Little League games or PTA meetings.

Zack took a noisy slurp of milk. "The best thing would be if you could meet some rich guy and marry him," he said. "Then we could go to Maui and stuff, like before. Or San Francisco, the skateboarders' paved heaven."

"Oh, Zack," she said tenderly. "I guess you're getting used to the idea of the divorce."

"What I'm not getting used to is the idea we can't have good stuff," said Zack.

"Listen to me," she said, narrowing her eyes. "Maybe it's a good thing we've had to retrench. It will be good for your character to realize you can't have whatever you want."

"You're pretty and nice," he said. "You could get a rich guy."

"Zack, that's horrible! How would you feel if someone married you for your money?"

"If she was pretty and nice it'd be a fair trade. Anyway, I have to get some first," he said. "I'm thinking of taking over Tyler's paper route."

"That sounds like a good idea," she said. "Then you can save up for a new skateboard whatever and that virtual thing you wanted."

"Virtual-reality helmet," Zack said. "Tyler says you get extra money if you sign up new people for the paper. Plus there's tips if you're like extra nice to the customers and don't throw the papers in the bushes and stuff."

Alice sighed. "Maybe KLEG should hire you to go out and sell advertising."

"Franklin," Caroline said dramatically, "I've met someone." The siblings were meeting in Franklin's office, where he was getting his sister to sign some tax forms relating to their mother's estate.

"Oh, really," he said casually, pretending not to get it. Of course Caroline didn't mean just anybody. She had met "somebody" with a capital *S*. She had met *a man*.

It was extraordinary. Franklin occasionally read the personals in the back of the *New York Review of Books* or in a local giveaway rag called the *Seattle Weekly*. There, self-styled female paragons—curvaceous, beautiful, cheerful, intelligent, witty women—declared themselves desperate and unable to meet guys.

Caroline, however, was never on the shelf for long, and advancing age hadn't seemed to slow her down one bit. She was certainly no looker. Franklin was sure he was right about that, even after taking into account the fact that she was his sister.

She wasn't particularly intelligent, either, being instead one of those rare but unfortunate people—Prince Charles was another example—who combined intellectual interests with stupidity. As for wit, Franklin's chief complaint about his sister was her complete lack of a sense of humor.

She was, however, keenly interested in men, although they were unfortunately of the wrong type. She also appeared to the world to be richer than she actually was, thanks to Dad's foresight in tying up her inheritance in a trust designed along the lines of a straitjacket.

The combination was deadly. Sleazy fortune hunters appeared with alarming regularity to court her. When they found out she had no access to her capital, they tended to fade away, although some had simply been carted off to rehab.

"Jeffrey's really a fascinating man," Caroline said girlishly. "And a wonderful artist."

Franklin felt irritation mingled with pity for his poor deluded sister. He also hoped he wouldn't have to socialize with Jeffrey.

Caroline always wanted her scruffy suitors to feel like one of the family.

"That's nice," said Franklin. "What kind of an artist is he?" While generally suspicious of all creative people, he felt that instrumental musicians and nonfiction writers were the least offensive. They actually had to know something or be able to do something useful. Actors and poets were at the bottom of the heap. Franklin considered most of them seriously disturbed people. He also felt that the less talent they had, the more likely they were to be riddled with character flaws and various kinds of dementia.

"He's a photographer. I was hoping you'd come and see his show next week. I'd love for you to meet him. He does trailer parks."

"You mean he shows at trailer parks?" asked Franklin. This was a new low.

"No, you idiot," snapped Caroline. "He photographs them. In fact, he's invited me down to Arizona on his next shoot. I was wondering if you could keep an eye on KLEG for me while I'm gone."

"Caroline, I have a real job! I do not have time to baby-sit those employees of yours so you can follow some man around through trailer parks. How well do you know this guy, anyway?"

"Pretty well," said Caroline. She raised one eyebrow knowingly, in the manner of Vivien Leigh as Scarlett O'Hara, and managed to produce an unpleasant leer.

Why couldn't she just pack it in and calm down? Mother hadn't been like this in her fifties. Why did these doctors have to stuff all these middle-aged women full of estrogen these days?

"Anyway," Caroline went on, "after we do the trailer parks— Jeffrey says they're every bit as depressing as Brazilian favelas or the slums of Bombay, although the impoverishment is more spiritual than material—we're going to spend a week or so at a spa down there, maybe get in a little tennis. Jeffrey really needs to unwind."

Yeah, on whose nickel? thought Franklin. The idea of this Jeffrey character playing tennis and knocking back cocktails at the swim-up bar while Franklin tried to keep order at KLEG was particularly galling. He made a noncommittal sound deep in his throat and changed the subject. "Here, sign this, Caroline. It's just a limited power of attorney. It authorizes me to straighten out this IRS screwup without bothering you."

Caroline said, "All right," in a petulant voice. As she signed, she said, "I really resent the fact that you won't let me have some time alone with someone I really care about. You don't give a damn about my feelings. You never have."

Watching his sister push the signed document back to him with a sulky twitch of her bony shoulders, Franklin had a sudden inspiration. "You're right, Caroline," he said, casting his eyes downward in what he hoped looked like an expression of contrition. "I've been selfish. Maybe on some level I'm envious of your happiness. Of course I'll keep an eye on things." He held up the paper she'd just signed. "We'll put together another one of these power of attorney things so I can take care of all the details while you're gone without bothering you."

"So what's the cause of death?" asked MacNab. Lukowski's brow was furrowed as he skimmed the medical examiner's report on Teresa Hoffman.

"Spontaneous natural death. That's what they call it when they just wear out and the ME's office is busy."

"So how old was she?" said MacNab.

"Ninety-seven. I've made an appointment to meet the next of kin over at the apartment. A grandniece from Oregon. Wanna come along?"

At Teresa Hoffman's apartment, the grandniece, Janet Wright, let them in. There were a few cardboard boxes sitting in the shabby little living room. Janet, a plump, freckled woman with a hearty, outdoorsy look, introduced her teenage daughter, Sara, who was standing in the living room staring at a flour sifter with bewilderment. "This must be some kind of an antique," she said. "I wonder what it was for?"

Her mother ignored her. "I can't imagine why you're interested in poor Aunt Teresa," she said to the detectives. "She'd had congestive heart failure for ages, and I'm afraid she was getting kind of out of it. We found lots of her pills tucked here and there. I don't think she was taking her medication."

"Actually," said Lukowski, "we wanted to talk to her about something else. It's part of a murder investigation."

Janet and Sara drew in their breath sharply.

It took Lukowski a while to explain who Teresa, Queen of the Night, was. He showed Janet the photocopies he'd made of canceled checks.

"That looks like her signature," said Janet. "I know it well because we wrote to each other pretty regularly. We used to talk on the phone before she got so deaf."

"Did she ever say anything about a radio program or about this Teresa, Queen of the Night, business?" asked MacNab.

"No. There must be some mistake."

"Is there anyone who might know what her connection was? Any friends or other relatives?"

"Not really. I'm afraid she outlived a lot of her friends."

"There's the guy upstairs," said Sara, pointing to the ceiling.

"Yes. This nice young man in an apartment on the second floor. He ran a lot of errands for her."

"Like maybe her banking?" said Lukowski.

"That's right. We met him just this morning. He was on his way to work. He was awfully sweet."

"What's this guy's name?" asked MacNab.

"I didn't get his name. Aunt Teresa wrote us about him, how he brought her groceries and stuff. She just called him the nice young man upstairs. Her legs would get so swollen it was hard for her to walk very far." The detectives were silent, and Janet Wright said defensively, "Naturally, I would have done more for her if I'd lived here in town."

Lukowski handed her a card. "When you see this guy again, have him call us. It's very important."

Outside the building, the detectives checked the names next to the doorbells. A C. Weeb lived on the second floor.

"Isn't that one of those nerds we ran into at the radio station?" asked MacNab.

CHAPTER FIFTEEN

The next morning, Alice was horrified to see that someone had been in her cubicle and gone through the papers there. She had definitely put a pile of leads right next to the phone. Now the pile was on the other side of the desk. The Rolodex was facing the wrong way, and the box of Ed Costello's papers looked different—as if everything had been taken out and put back in reverse order.

She immediately suspected Judy. Perhaps the surly receptionist wasn't content with simply eavesdropping on phone calls. Alice was highly indignant. It was unreasonable to be expected to work under these conditions. Now that she had made a couple of sales, she felt bold enough to complain to Caroline, but Caroline, as usual, was nowhere to be found.

Maybe she should confront Judy directly. She glanced over the cubicle wall toward the reception desk and the back of Judy's head. No, she realized she didn't have the stomach for it. Judy had a ruthless, self-righteous quality that scared her. Maybe she should do something sneaky, like smear rancid bacon fat all over Judy's vegetarian organic lunch.

Alice told herself to calm down and not to sink to the depths in which Judy herself apparently wallowed. Instead, she walked slowly over to the receptionist's desk and said with a carefully contrived puzzled expression, "You know, Judy, I actually believe someone has gone through my desk. My papers seem to have been shifted around slightly."

"Why are you telling me about it?" said Judy angrily. "Do you think I would do something like that?"

"Of—of course not," stammered Alice. "It just seems weird."

"Listen," said Judy with her usual irritating self-importance. "That Detective Lukowski is coming around to talk to some of the staff in about an hour. I may have some important information to discuss with him, and I'll be conferring with him privately. Could you get the phones?"

"I'm sorry, but I don't have time," said Alice. "Why don't you turn on the machine?" She knew exactly how people like Judy operated. Help them out with their job once as a favor, and next thing you knew they expected it all the time.

Alice was excited. The detective in charge of Ed Costello's case was coming around in person.

Just then Caroline walked into the office with a seedy-looking man in a frayed and battered tweed jacket. "Here it is," she said to him. "My baby, KLEG." She gestured at the pathetic surroundings, then introduced Alice and Judy. "This is Jeffrey Fleming, a very important photographer with a fabulous show coming up."

"Wow," said Jeffrey, holding his hands in front of his eyes in a little square and squinting. "I wouldn't mind taking some pictures here." He had the yellowing plastic busts of Bach and Beethoven and the dying plants in his sights, then swung around to frame Judy and the dented file cabinet behind her.

"Jeffrey usually takes pictures of decrepit trailer parks and emotionally disturbed people," explained Caroline, unconscious of any irony. "I brought him in so someone can interview him. I guess Daphne is on the air now, right?"

Judy compressed her mouth into a disapproving line. "You'd better speak to Phil about any schedule changes," she said. "After all, he is the program director. And we do publish our listener guide. It won't have anything about an interview with him." She pointed at the interloper.

"I'm sure we can arrange all this with Phil," said Caroline, taking Jeffrey Fleming by the hand and leading him away. "Follow me, darling."

Judy leaped at the phone on her desk and jabbed at a few buttons. "Phil! Caroline's coming your way with her new squeeze," she whispered hoarsely into the phone. "She wants Daphne to do a live interview with him right now. Hang in there. Don't let her push you around. Remember, you're the program director, not her!" She replaced the receiver with a gimlety look of triumph.

Daphne, well into Debussy's *La Mer*, drifted into the reception area. She was carrying a lipstick and a compact. "God!" she said. "What happened in the bathroom?"

"I don't know," said Judy angrily. "I'm not in charge of the bathroom." Alice remembered that Franklin had suggested she clean it.

"The window's broken, and there's glass all over the floor. The mirror's still intact, though." She grabbed a tissue from Judy's desk and blotted her scarlet lips.

"Tell Caroline," said Judy. "Oh, by the way, she wants you to interview her new boyfriend. Some kind of a photographer.

Probably another gigolo after her money. He's definitely younger."

"What happened to her old boyfriend?" said Daphne. "That puppeteer?"

"Last I overheard, she told him he was too controlling," said Judy confidentially. "She accused him of treating her like one of his puppets, and then they had a big fight about his getting his junk out of her house. He said he didn't have anyplace to put it because he had to move back in with his mom in her little retirement apartment. I actually heard him start to sob. You know, a little catch in the throat? So Caroline left all his stuff in her driveway with a plastic tarp over it, but he claimed that it all got wet anyway, and then—" Judy cut off her report as a tall man with a tanned face and a shock of prematurely white hair came in and presented himself at her desk.

This must be the detective. Alice liked the look of him immediately. He was more attractive than any of the real-life detectives she'd seen on her beloved *Cops* or testifying on *Court TV*.

Judy gave Detective Lukowski the nicest—perhaps the only—smile Alice had ever seen her produce. "Oh, hi," she said. "I guess you'll want to talk to me."

"Um, well actually," he said, "I was hoping to have a word with Carl Weeb first."

"Carl?" Judy looked surprised and disappointed.

"Are you the detective trying to find out whatever happened to poor Ed?" said Daphne, favoring Lukowski with a heavy-lidded vampy look. "I'm Daphne Hamilton. Perhaps you've heard me on the air. I'll take you to Carl." He followed her swaying hips down the corridor toward the record library.

Alice resolved to stick around until he finished talking to Carl. She wanted to tell him she thought someone might have broken into the station last night through the bathroom window and gone through Ed Costello's papers.

In his law office, Franklin was amusing himself by writing a series of pompous, harassing memos, which he intended to distribute to the KLEG staff in his sister's absence:

To: All on-air staff
From: Franklin Payne, acting station manager

In future, announcers will spell out the station's call letters. KLEG sounds like "cleg" which my *OED* tells me is a horsefly or gadfly (Old Norse: *kleggi*). Even if the meaning is unknown to most listeners, KLEG pronounced phonetically is not euphonious. I'm well aware that my late mother, whose maiden name was Klegg, named the station after herself, but even she agreed it wasn't a particularly attractive name. Thank you for your cooperation.

Rereading the memo gave him grim satisfaction, and he launched into his second effort:

I have noticed that announcers are referring to "Ludwig van Beethoven" and "Wolfgang Amadeus Mozart." This strikes me as patronizing to our listeners and makes you seem like pretentious little half-educated jerks. I'm sure none of you would want to create such an impression.

For God's sake, of course it was Ludwig van Beethoven who wrote Beethoven's Ninth. Who else could it have been, his cousin Fritz Beethoven?

Please use first names only for more obscure composers
or—as in the case of the Strausses, for instance—when there
are multiple composers of the same last name. When referring to Johann Sebastian Bach, simply say "Bach," unless of
course you mean less important members of the Bach family,
such as Johann Christian.

Under no circumstances, as I have heard you do, refer to
Haydn (Franz Joseph, not Michael, of course) as "Papa
Haydn."

Feeling that he was on a roll, Franklin began a third memo.

To: All staff
Re: Personal hygiene and beach attire in the workplace.

Daphne led Lukowski into the record library. "Here's Carl,"
she said. She touched the detective's elbow and lowered her
thickly mascaraed lashes. "I'll be in the broadcast booth if you
need to talk to me," she said. "Just make sure the On Air sign is
off."

"Fine," said Lukowski, nodding at Carl, who stared at him
through his screen of greasy hair. In the corner of the room an
older man seemed to be arguing with a bucktoothed middle-
aged woman, while a guy in a beat-up Harris Tweed jacket stood
by.

"I'm sorry," the old guy was saying. "I can't let management
usurp the authority of the programming staff when it comes to
what actually goes out over the airwaves."

"But, Phil," the woman said, "we need more coverage of the
arts in general. That was Mother's vision. A world-class voice for
the cultural life of Seattle."

The combatants ignored Lukowski. He turned to Carl. "Is there somewhere quiet where we can talk?" he asked.

Carl nodded silently, came out from behind his desk and led Lukowski back down the hall to the break room. His rubber flip-flops made slapping noises on the linoleum.

"What's up?" he said in a shy little voice, leaning on the old chrome dinette table, his arms crossed defensively.

Lukowski assumed a more aggressive posture, with his hands on his hips. "We're looking for Teresa, Queen of the Night. Your neighbor, Teresa Hoffman, cashed her checks from KLEG, apparently with your help. What the hell's going on?"

"Okay, okay," said Carl nervously. "I'll try to arrange a meeting. Teresa, Queen of the Night, calls me every couple of days to talk programming. I told her about your card when I found it in Miss Hoffman's door. Did she get in touch?"

"What's the deal here anyway?" demanded Lukowski. "You got a phone number for her? An address?"

"Yeah, well, not really. I've never actually met her. No one has. She's really determined to be anonymous. So I fixed it that when I took Miss Hoffman's Social Security check to the bank, I got her to endorse the KLEG check too, and I cashed it. Then I put the cash in an envelope and mailed it to the real Teresa's post office box."

"This doesn't make any sense at all," said Lukowski. "How did you get the check in the first place?"

"Teresa collects it. Then mails it to me. Then I get Miss Hoffman to endorse it. Then I send her the cash back."

"Come on. Give me a break," said Lukowski.

"I swear to God, it's true," said Carl in a defensive whine.

"Now that Teresa Hoffman is dead, what are you going to do?"

"I don't know," said Carl. "I'm waiting for the other Teresa to tell me."

"This is very screwy," said Lukowski. "Do you have any idea why this individual is so reluctant to come forward?"

"I've thought about that a lot," said Carl pensively. "In fact, she's kind of hinted she's in one of those federal protected witness programs. You know. Like she was some Mafia guy's girl-friend or something." Carl paused and Lukowski gave him a skeptical look. "Hey, it made sense to me," said Carl, with the first hint of aggression. "She pronounces Italian really well. She back-announces all those arias beautifully."

"Oh, really? Listen, when she calls, tell her if she doesn't come forward, the police will find her. All we want to do is ask her a few questions about Ed Costello." Lukowski stepped a little closer to Carl, who looked startled and bolted sideways against the edge of the dinette table like a frightened animal.

Lukowski raised his voice a little. "And I advise you to coop-erate with us yourself, Mr. Weeb. This is a homicide investiga-tion. We don't have time to play games. You talk to her and get back to me or Detective MacNab as soon as you speak to her."

Lukowski thrust another card at Carl, then left the break room fuming. If he couldn't flush this witness out, he'd have to put someone on a stakeout by the P.O. box for days. The expense would be pretty hard to justify. He didn't even know if this Teresa had anything of value to contribute to the investigation. All he knew was that she was avoiding him and wasting his time.

He frowned at Judy, who accosted him as soon as he emerged back into the reception area. "I left you a message about Franklin Payne and the escort service," Judy stage-whispered. Carl Weeb scuttled past them both, his head down, his face ob-scured once more by his limp hair, and Judy maneuvered

Lukowski back into the break room. "Let me tell you all about it."

"Okay," he said.

"Well," said Judy urgently, "Franklin was carrying on, complaining about the station like he always does, and he said now that Ed's escort service was gone, we'd lost the only profit center we had around here. That sounded to me like he was getting some of the profits."

"I see," said Lukowski. "You're sure he wasn't just kidding around?"

"Kidding? You mean like a joke?" said Judy with a puzzled frown.

"Yeah," said Lukowski. "People kid around, you know. To amuse each other." This woman struck him as less than a million laughs. "Did Mr. Payne sound like he was kidding or joking?"

"I didn't actually hear him," answered Judy. "Phil did."

"We'll look into it," said Lukowski. "Now if you'll excuse me . . ." He strode purposefully toward the door.

Waiting outside the break room this time was yet another employee. He'd noticed her when he came in. She was a sweet-faced, rosy-looking woman.

"If you don't mind," she said in a deferential little voice, "there's something I think you should know. My name is Alice Jordan and—"

"Oh, yeah," interrupted Lukowski. "You left me a message with the license-plate number of that Corvette. Thanks. We appreciated it."

Alice Jordan looked thrilled to have been helpful. Behind him, Judy said testily, "What Corvette? What's this all about?"

Lukowski turned and looked at her for a second, but didn't bother to answer, then turned his attention back to Alice.

"You see," began Alice, "I took over for Ed Costello, and I have all his papers on my desk. Last night someone went through them. I believe they gained entry by breaking the bathroom window."

"Really? Let's take a look."

Alice took him into a spartan little bathroom that also seemed to function as a broom closet. Stuffed in with the toilet, sink and medicine cabinet were some mops and brooms, a vacuum cleaner and a gallon of some industrial cleaning agent. A few mummified rags hung from the exposed elbow pipe beneath the wall-mounted sink. Judging by the look of the KLEG offices, and especially this room, Lukowski surmised that the cleaning equipment didn't get much of a workout.

There were shards of glass in the sink and all over the floor. The window was clearly big enough to allow someone to get into the building. "Let's see your desk," said Lukowski, backing out of the bathroom.

Alice Jordan took him to her cubicle and pointed out that things had been moved around. Lukowski recognized the box of papers. He'd made copies of everything in there before returning it to Franklin Payne.

"Anything missing?"

"I've tried to figure that out," said Alice. Her eyes got wider and she said rather breathlessly, "I thought I shouldn't go through the papers in case the intruder's fingerprints were on them. I didn't want to contaminate the scene."

Lukowski smiled at her. This woman clearly read a lot of detective stories or true crime books. Even the way she phrased things—"gained entry," "contaminate the scene"—indicated she was a cop buff. Maybe she was even a genteel version of a cop groupie, a species known to every police officer. "That was smart," he said.

A smile blossomed on her face. "It occurred to me," she went on eagerly, "that seeing as Mr. Costello was apparently operating a vice ring, maybe one of the customers might have been looking for any evidence that might reveal his involvement."

Lukowski thought the same thing. "I'll get some technicians down here to go over the bathroom and these papers for fingerprints," he said. He would also compare his photocopies of Ed's papers with what was still here in the box to see what, if anything, was missing.

Most murders that got solved were solved quickly. This was trickier. It was the kind of case mystery fans and cop buffs like Alice Jordan loved but cops hated. Lukowski hoped that this apparent break-in might get the investigation moving at last.

He leaned toward her and said dramatically, in his best TV detective's manner, "You better not touch anything here until the boys from the lab can go over it all." He was rewarded by the look of pure delight on Alice's face.

CHAPTER SIXTEEN

Back in his office in the Public Safety building, Lukowski was startled to hear from MacNab that Teresa had called and arranged to be questioned.

"That was fast," said Lukowski. "Maybe that Weeb dweeb knows more than he lets on. When's she coming in?"

"Well, actually," said MacNab, looking slightly embarrassed, "she insisted we meet for a drink. Just her and me. She said Carl said you were pretty aggressive and she felt I would be more sympathetic."

"What? And you went for that?"

"Well, seeing as she's so shy and all—"

"Oh, come on! Don't tell me you're buying into that Greta Garbo routine! I suppose it was that fuck-me voice of hers."

"Maybe it was," said MacNab with a thoughtful look.

"Have you heard her on the radio? She's some kind of a nymphomaniac. Just the kind of sicko who'd file sexual harassment charges or something. I wouldn't talk to her without a witness."

"We're meeting at the Retro Room at five."

"What did I tell you? That little cock tease chose the darkest bar in town," sneered Lukowski.

"Yeah, you're right," said MacNab. "You better come along. There's definitely something weird about her."

"If you ask me," said Lukowski, "all those people at KLEG are one taco short of a combination plate." He mentally made an exception for Alice Jordan. Too bad a nice woman like that had to work in a place like KLEG.

Normally, Franklin would have avoided meeting his sister's new lover for as long as possible, but he was so eager to get her out of the picture that he'd agreed to give Caroline and Jeffrey Fleming a ride to the airport. He was going to pick them up at KLEG, and he planned to begin terrorizing the staff immediately.

When he arrived, Caroline seemed to be having some sort of flap with Phil Bernard. They were snapping at each other in her office. A man he presumed was Jeffrey Fleming was reading a magazine in the waiting area. Judy scowled at Franklin from the reception desk, and Alice Jordan seemed to be doing something at a filing cabinet across the room, pretending not to hear the raised voices of Phil and Caroline through the glass door.

Phil trailing her, Caroline rushed out to the waiting area and introduced Franklin to Jeffrey. She beamed at them both. "I hope you'll be good friends," she gushed. "I'm so fond of you both." Franklin never understood why Caroline always got a big surge of family feeling when she had a new man in her life. Franklin had always been very careful to protect any woman he cared about from his relatives for as long as possible.

Jeffrey gave Franklin a big, eager smile, and Franklin gave Jeffrey a frostier, smaller one in return. Caroline was running true to form: Fleming looked dissipated, shifty and impoverished.

Phil, hovering at Caroline's elbow, said peevishly, "I'm afraid I must stand my ground here."

"What's going on?" demanded Franklin.

"Phil doesn't want to run an interview with Jeffrey right now," said Caroline. "He says we have to stick by the program guide."

Franklin turned to Phil. "Why don't you tape it for broadcast later?" he said. He turned to his sister. "Have you told the staff?"

"Told us what?" said Judy shrilly from her desk. Alice Jordan looked up from the filing cabinet.

"Get everyone in here," said Franklin sternly. "We'll make an official announcement." He savored the idea that for the few moments it took to round them all up, they'd be suffering from feelings of impending doom.

When Caroline had managed to collect them all—Carl, Phil, Daphne, Alice and Judy were present and accounted for—Franklin said, "Caroline will be gone for a while on a much deserved month-long vacation in Arizona. I will be acting station manager in her absence. You can expect to see me around here quite a bit, making sure things are operating smoothly. I'm really looking forward to the opportunity to have some input here." He reached into his inside pocket, came up with his collection of insulting staff memos and flung them at Judy. "Type these up and circulate them," he said. Then he glanced around the offices. "You know, this place could use a good cleaning. Maybe you can get some kind of a work party together and put your backs into it while I run my sister and her new friend to the airport."

"We should wait until the lab boys have been here and gone," said Alice eagerly. "There will probably be fingerprint powder all over everything."

The two detectives groped their way through a sea of small, round chrome-legged tables, guided only by a few tiny candles in red glass containers. "Jesus," muttered Lukowski, who had once acted in a high school production of *The Pajama Game,* "this place is a regular Hernando's Hideaway." The Retro Room was riding a wave of nostalgia for the fabulous fifties. Perry Como crooned from the speakers, large trapezoidal ashtrays indicated that smoking was encouraged, and martinis were the specialty of the house.

"That far corner table," said MacNab, pointing. "That's where she said to meet her."

Lukowski nodded. "Okay. She might bolt if she sees two of us. I'll wait at the bar. As soon as she sits down, I'll come over and we can corner her. All I can say is, after this buildup she better have something interesting to say."

"I wonder what she looks like," said MacNab rather wistfully. "Think you can tell much from a voice?"

"If she had a face and body to match that voice," said Lukowski, "she wouldn't be hiding out all the time." He went over to the bar and ordered a pint of a microbrew on tap.

A few minutes later a young woman came into the bar. From what Lukowski could see in the dark, she wore a short black dress with sheer black seamed stockings and high heels. She had a mane of dark hair about shoulder length, which she flipped over her shoulder as she made her way languorously toward MacNab. In keeping with the general tone of the Retro Room, she also wore a small black satin pillbox cocktail hat with a half-veil.

A trio of businessmen huddled over a small table looked up as she passed. She had a confident, slow, sexy stride that seemed to be screaming, "Eat your heart out." Lukowski watched her favor the men with a knowing smile as she passed. Conversation at the table ceased and they all craned around to check out her fabulous legs.

Lukowski waited until she sat down across from MacNab, took a cigarette out of a small handbag, handed a lighter to MacNab so that he'd light her cigarette, leaned into the flame as he held it up for her, then settled back against the red leather banquette, shooting a plume of silver smoke through her veil up to the ceiling. Lukowski grabbed his beer and went over to the corner table.

"This is my partner, Detective Lukowski," said MacNab. "Teresa here says she doesn't have a last name."

"Everyone has a last name," said Lukowski, indicating she should shove over to make room for him. She gave him a startled look, then scrunched over and made a big deal of crossing her legs, revealing an expanse of taut thigh.

"Look," said MacNab, "we want to know what you know about Ed Costello and the Home Run Escort Service. Your voice was on his tape."

"It's just like I told you when I called and left a message with Detective Lukowski here," said Teresa in her come-hither voice. This was Teresa, Queen of the Night, all right. "I thought it was all a joke. Honestly, I never met the man in my life." She made a fluttery, helpless little gesture and flexed her head back to exhale more smoke. Lukowski's eyes followed the line of her long, pale neck, and then he checked out her face. It was heavily made up, but stunning, with fine bones and sultry eyes smoldering

through the black lace of the veil. It also looked strangely familiar.

"I've got a question for you, Teresa," he said. "What size shoes
do you wear?" He looked under the table at her feet. She was
wearing black suede high heels with a lot of tarty-looking straps
over the instep.

"Shoes?" She smiled and blinked furiously. Her Minnie
Mouse eyelashes looked fake. "Oh, that's right. Carl said they
found a pair of shoes at the station. Not mine, I assure you."

"No, I guess not. I'd say you wear about a twelve. A man's
twelve. Probably the same size as Carl Weeb."

MacNab looked startled, and Lukowski saw him glance down
at her hands, which had shiny coffee-colored nails. She folded
them up, but not quickly enough. They were big and square,
with pronounced knuckles.

"In fact," said Lukowski, "you are Carl Weeb, aren't you?"
Teresa's face crumpled. In a reassuring tone that he summoned
up whenever he was confronted with hurt female feelings,
Lukowski went on, "Hey, you look fabulous. If I hadn't talked
to your, um, other personality earlier today, I never would have
guessed." He was too kind to mention the fact that his first clue
had been an Adam's apple sliding around on top of that elegant
neck as Teresa exhaled her cigarette smoke.

"Oh, hell," said Teresa, stubbing out her half-smoked cigarette
rather viciously. She turned to MacNab and sighed. "I asked
you to come alone. I would have pulled it off if you'd come
alone."

MacNab looked blustery, as if he was about to sputter that
he hadn't been fooled. Lukowski doubted that, judging by the
goofy look he'd had while lighting her cigarette. To stay on

Teresa's good side, Lukowski said gallantly, "We both wanted to meet the famous Teresa."

"Look," she said, "is there any reason you have to tell anyone down at KLEG about this? I've got a fabulous following, but Phil Bernard is adamant about keeping poor mousy little Carl off the air."

"Your secret is safe with us," said Lukowski.

"But only if you're straight, um, straightforward with us," added MacNab.

Teresa sighed again. "All right. I recorded that answering-machine tape because that slimebag Ed Costello made me do it. He found out that I was really Carl and said he'd tell if I didn't." Teresa reached inside her neckline and delicately adjusted a bra strap. "I'd sure like a martini."

Lukowski signaled a waitress and ordered it for her.

"Bombay gin, very dry, two olives," she added.

"How did Ed find out?" said MacNab.

Teresa wrinkled her nose. "Stupid me. I got sloppy one night, and my tape was short. I sneaked in to do the last half hour live. I'd done it before. It's kind of a kick to work live. Anyway, Ed came in a little later to tend to his escort business. He heard my voice over the speakers in the office and saw the On Air light was on and looked through the glass and saw Carl sitting there with my voice coming out of his mouth."

"You mean you weren't all dressed up like now?" said MacNab. Lukowski sensed that the literal-minded MacNab was struggling with gender issues and couldn't conceive of Carl being transformed into Teresa without full wardrobe and makeup.

Teresa laughed. "The magic of radio. No one knows what you're wearing. A girl might as well be comfortable. Anyway, I begged him not to tell. He took a sadistic pleasure in having something on me. It was very chilling. He asked me what it was worth to me to keep my secret.

"While we were arguing about it, I heard his answering machine come on. He'd thought he was alone, too, and he'd turned up the speaker on the machine. He had one of his tarts reading his message."

"So you both had something on each other," summarized Lukowski.

"That's right. When I heard his machine, I told him I'd keep my mouth shut about his operation if he wouldn't snitch to Phil about Teresa's true identity. Then, for good measure, I told him the tape sounded really tacky." She rolled her eyes. "Some squeaky little low-class slut trying to sound classy."

Teresa's martini arrived. She took a sip and produced a satisfied little purr. "Ed said he hoped there were no hard feelings, and he promised not to tell on me. Then he asked really nicely if I'd record a new message for him. More professional-sounding. I thought it would keep him sweet, and kind of smooth over the fact that we were blackmailing each other." Teresa smiled. "But just in case, I got absolute proof of what he was up to."

"Absolute proof?"

"That's right." Teresa looked pleased with herself. "I taped him in his cubicle, running his escort business."

"You taped him?" Lukowski was interested. "How?"

"Your basic twenty-dollar voice-activated tape recorder from Radio Shack. I put it under his desk for a couple of nights. You can hear his half of the conversation while he answers the messages on his machine. I just listened to the first five minutes, and I knew I had him. There was no doubt about what he was up to."

"You still have the tape?" asked MacNab.

"Sure. It's at home. But I guess I don't need it anymore."

"We'd like to listen to it," said Lukowski. "Can we run you home and pick it up?"

"Actually," said Teresa, consulting a small gold watch, "I'm meeting someone for dinner. I don't like to be more than a little late on a first date." Teresa smiled. "He's a retired Marine Corps officer. Probably likes everything neat and punctual. I could bring the tape to work tomorrow. Can you pick it up there? Discreetly?"

Lukowski was irritated. Teresa should just cooperate, like any good citizen. This was a police investigation, for God's sake. To his surprise, MacNab said, "Okay. Don't want to keep an officer and a gentleman waiting."

After she'd left, Lukowski muttered, "We should've made her break that date. God, MacNab, anyone bats his or her eyelashes at you like that, and you just fold."

"Old interservice rivalry," said MacNab with a smug little smile. "I never did like those jarheads I had to cross-train with years ago. I'm betting that guy doesn't know he's meeting a chick with a dick."

"Maybe he'll figure it out right away," said Lukowski, reflecting on the size-twelve pumps.

MacNab bristled a little at this suggestion. "I think Teresa is too much of a lady to get intimate on the first date," he said.

CHAPTER SEVENTEEN

Stan Edgecombe had been everything Teresa had hoped for. Sweet. Understanding. So respectful. Just the kind of old-fashioned guy she thought didn't exist anymore. She'd practically had to put him in an armlock just to give him a little peck on the cheek at the door. And he'd been so darling, telling her he had to run home and listen to Teresa, Queen of the Night.

Sighing happily, she turned on the stereo and listened to her own voice announcing a Puccini aria, then kicked off her heels and collapsed in a beanbag chair in the middle of her apartment. After a second, she remembered she'd promised to give those detectives the tape she'd made of Ed Costello. She wondered if there was anything interesting on it, past the five minutes or so she'd heard before. It might be worth a listen before parting with it.

She rose again, found the cassette, put it in the machine, pulled off her wig and went into the bathroom to get ready for bed. While she was peeling off her lashes, Ed's voice came rumbling out into the apartment.

"No problem," he was saying. "We'll have Dagmar and Candy out there in half an hour." There was a pause. "No problem."

Another pause. "Well, maybe. I can't guarantee that. You'll have to negotiate that with the girls themselves. I can tell you one thing." Here, Ed chuckled. "It'll cost you a lot extra."

Teresa curled her lip in disgust and rubbed cold cream into her face, creating a glassy palette of smeared beige foundation, burgundy lipstick, raspberry blusher and charcoal eye shadow.

The machine turned itself off when there was silence and kicked in again when it heard something. Right after the sound of telephone buttons being tapped, Ed came on again, sending two of his girls out to an address in the University District. "The guy has some very specific requests. He's got a couple of outfits for you gals to wear. There are a lot of feathers involved, and he wants to make sure neither of you are allergic. Apparently he can't keep it up when people are sneezing around him."

Teresa, now looking like Carl again, brushed his teeth, and wondered what the guy in the U District had in mind. All he could come up with was Papageno and Papagena outfits from Carl's own favorite opera, *The Magic Flute,* and maybe a giant birdcage with a swinging perch or something.

More phone blips, and Ed's voice again. "Good," he said. "I'm glad you agree that this is best for everyone. Fine. Cash. Great. Well, I know you want to be discreet. We can meet at the radio station after hours. Call me when you have it all together."

There was a slight pause and then Ed said in a defensive voice: "Blackmail is a little harsh. Think of it as security. And cheap at the price. A thousand bucks. Big deal. It's a onetime-only fee." Ed chuckled again, then said in a slightly hurt voice, "Yeah, well everyone's trying to make a buck. What can I tell you? There's nothing personal here. Okay. Good-bye."

Ed hung up and gave a little laugh of triumph, then began

singing "My Way" in an off-key rendition that nonetheless reflected a familiarity with Sinatra's phrasing.

What a sleaze, thought Carl. Whoever Ed had been putting the squeeze on there, he'd expressed the same glum, smug, evil pleasure in having some kind of knowledge about them as he had when he tumbled to Carl's own secret. What a contrast Ed Costello was with someone upright and straightforward and honest and decent like Stanton Edgecombe.

Ed was back on the phone, in hyper-salesman mode. "Yeah. Boy, these girls are really hot," he was saying. "They get restless and horny on their days off. Seriously. They're so eager I have to remind them to collect the money. I swear to God. You know, if they didn't need to earn a living, I bet they'd do what they do for free, they love it so much. And it shows in their work, you better believe it."

Disgusted, Carl unzipped his dress, stepped out of it and went over to turn off the tape. This kind of thing was a travesty of real feeling. There were fine men like Stanton Edgecombe around who were genuinely interested in a decent, loving relationship. Carl had begun to doubt this, but after this evening, his faith in the possibility of true love had been slightly restored.

As he was about to turn off the machine, Carl was startled to hear Bob LeBaron's voice. "Hi, Ed, how's it going? Still selling nooky out of your cubicle?" He laughed expansively.

"Just trying to help out a few lonely guys," responded Ed.

"Yeah, well, I guess some guys have to pay for it," Bob said smugly. "By the way, Ed, you got those Sonics tickets for me?"

Carl turned off the tape. Apparently Bob LeBaron knew what Ed was up to. He'd have to, really, seeing as Bob was on from six to midnight.

It was all so pathetic. Those washed-up losers from the

Golden Age of radio cluttering things up, not to mention Phil.
None of them understood that he, Carl, could make that station
into a really exciting place. He'd have to be content with Teresa's
shift. For now, anyway.

KLEG could be a really cool station, he just knew it. All it
needed was some panache. A few years from now, when digital-
ized AM came online, the music quality could be as good as
FM, and the station could really take off. Instead, KLEG was
just a depressing little byway, staffed by unfeeling jerks, none of
whom appreciated Carl and his true sense of style. Life was so
unfair.

Alice was surprised to see Franklin in Caroline's office the
next morning when she came in. The glass door was closed and
he was on the phone with his feet on the desk. Apparently he
had meant it when he said he was going to take an interest in the
station. At the reception desk, Judy put the phone down hastily.
Alice assumed she'd been monitoring Franklin's phone call. In a
matter-of-fact tone designed to catch her off guard, Alice said,
"So who's he talking to now?"

"Just his law office," said Judy. She curled her lip. "His secretary is so deferential. It's disgusting."

Alice summoned up her nerve. "Listen, I've been out of the
workforce for some time and maybe I've forgotten how things
are done, but it seems a little odd that you listen in on people's
phone calls. I really hope you aren't listening to mine."

The two women fell silent as Franklin emerged from Caroline's office and walked over to the studio.

"I'm not saying whether or not I listen to phone calls per-
taining to station business," said Judy when he was gone. "I don't

think that's any of your concern. Anyway, when I was a telemarketer management listened in."

Alice gave her a skeptical look and said, "But you knew that, right?"

Judy didn't answer and changed tack. "Technically, the French Resistance was an illegal operation. There are times when rules must be broken for a greater good. There's such a thing as a higher morality. Keep in mind that special circumstances call for drastic measures."

"What's so special about the circumstances here?" asked Alice.

Judy leaned over to her and said in a fierce whisper, "You don't understand. The very future of KLEG may be on the line. We have proof that Franklin wants to sell the station. Caroline may be in on it with him."

"Well, they own it, don't they?" said Alice. She didn't ask how Judy's eavesdropping could stop them in any case.

"KLEG isn't just *any* business," said Judy. "It's a part of Seattle's cultural heritage. Why should they be able to do with it what they like? We work here. You too. We could all be out on the street."

Alice wondered how long she'd have to be on the payroll to get unemployment compensation if they were all fired. "Ethical considerations aside, Judy, I hope you're not listening to my phone calls. That would make me very uncomfortable."

"Yeah, well, don't snitch to management, Alice," said Judy. She reached out and grabbed Alice's wrist and said in an ominous tone, "Remember what happened to Ed."

"Let go of me!" Alice said loudly, just as Franklin emerged from the studio. She regretted raising her voice. She was afraid she sounded like a bad actress in a catfight scene from some cheap girls'-reform-school melodrama.

"Ladies, please!" Franklin said, bustling over. "What's going on here?" He was carrying a hammer and a piece of plywood.

"Nothing," said Judy in a low snarl, withdrawing her hand.

Alice resented the way Franklin had said "ladies"—plural—as if she were just as nuts as Judy. "I'm sorry. Judy just startled me," she said, hustling off to her cubicle. If only she had a real office with a door, like a grown-up, she could close it and put her head down on the desk and weep a little.

Franklin turned to Judy. "Try not to scare the other employees," he said. "And please call a staff meeting for eleven this morning. Everyone. Get Bob LeBaron out of bed, too." He went over to Alice's cubicle.

Alice was afraid Franklin was going to ask her what she and Judy were squabbling about. Instead, he gave her a nice smile, unlike the sharklike gloating smile she'd seen on his face before. "Say, Alice, I saw those contracts. You actually sold something. Good work."

"Thanks," she said. It was the first kind word she'd had from anyone at KLEG since coming to work here.

"I have a little assignment for you," he continued. "We've got a lot of electronic equipment here, and after that break-in, I realized we need better security. See if you can find a burglar-alarm company that's willing to do a trade." He held up the plywood. "I found this in the studio. This is our security for now, until you can work out a trade."

"A trade?"

"That's right. We'll run ads in return for them installing a security system. We'll pay you the same commission you would have gotten if they paid real money."

"Okay," said Alice.

"The police tell me the intruders were only interested in your cubicle, thank God. Anything missing?"

"I was curious about that myself, but I didn't want to go through the things until the police had finished dusting for prints," she said. "Ed's box of papers was definitely gone through."

"I'm curious, too," said Franklin. "Bring that box into my office and we'll examine it together after I finish with the window."

After a period of loud banging, Franklin came out of the bathroom, looking proud of himself. Daphne was reading a public service announcement about lost pets, her voice trembling with emotion. Franklin handed the hammer to Judy. "Put that back in the toolbox in the studio when she stops talking."

He and Alice went into his office and got to work. "It's kind of like Kim's game, you know?" she said as they went through the items in the box.

"Oh, yeah. That Kipling thing where you have to remember everything on a tray. They used to make us do that in Boy Scouts," said Franklin. He held up Chip's phone number and gazed at it with a shudder.

Alice caught his glance. "Oh," she said. "I called that guy. He had a weird message on his machine."

"I know," said Franklin, tossing the number in the wastebasket. "He's completely nuts. I hope you didn't talk to him."

"Not exactly," she replied. "I left a message, asking him if he wanted to advertise."

"Forget it!" said Franklin. "There are some people even KLEG is too proud to do business with."

"I wonder what Ed Costello was doing with Chip's number," mused Alice.

"Some flaky scheme of Ed's, no doubt." Alice noticed that Franklin looked embarrassed, perhaps because of his association, however slight, with the late Ed Costello.

She held up the file marked "Leads" and felt its weight. "You know, I think whatever's missing was in here. It seems to me this was heavier." She opened the folder. "Wasn't there some kind of a booklet?" She closed her eyes to concentrate. "A stapled thing," she said in a dreamy tone like some psychic grasping for a flash of truth. "Newsprint . . ."

Franklin looked through the file. "That catalog," he said, handing it back to her. "The mail-order bride thing. Remember?"

"You're absolutely right," said Alice, flipping through the file once more. They looked at each other with smiles of triumph.

CHAPTER EIGHTEEN

"The prints on the broken glass were definitely this Charles Gilmore guy's." MacNab was filling Lukowski in on the fingerprint technician's report.

"Thank God for that computer," said Lukowski. He remembered the old days, when the only way you could get a match was to have a suspect already. Now, thanks to the voters of King County, any set of prints already on file in the computer could be immediately matched with a sample.

"Yeah. Charles Gilmore. Great military genius and criminal mastermind," said MacNab, shaking his head. "Too stupid to wear gloves."

"We better go talk to Chip," said Lukowski. "Anybody got a good address on him?"

"Yeah, but he's not home," said MacNab. "I called my buddy over at the FBI. Chip's in Idaho at a home schooling and gun show until day after tomorrow. Anyway, we got him on breaking and entering. That should be good enough to get a search warrant and see what we can find over at his place."

"It looks like what was taken was this," said Lukowski, waving a sheaf of Xerox copies. He handed it to his partner. "I'd rather not tip him off just yet that we found out he was the one who broke in. Not until we know more."

"Huh?" said MacNab. "Mail-order brides? I don't get it." He flipped through the Xerox copies of the catalog pages. "Boy, you'd have to be pretty hard up to do this, wouldn't you? I guess the idea is you get a wife who's guaranteed not to bust your balls."

"Speaking of which," said Lukowski, "I think it's time we had another talk with Mrs. Costello. I'd like to know what she knows about Charles W. Gilmore. Let's do that on our way over to get that tape from Teresa at the station."

"Gee, I hadn't thought about Chip Gilmore in years." Lorraine Costello was showing Lukowski and MacNab an old photo album. "See? There he is. Kind of a quiet type. The engineers were always kind of quiet. Just the opposite of the sales department. We were wild and crazy." She smiled nostalgically.

She pointed out a shot of what appeared to be a party scene. A group of people sat around a table, some of them toasting the camera with plastic cups. Everyone's eyes were bright red. "There's me and Ed, and Chip, and a couple of gals who worked with me in Sales Support. We scheduled all the spots. And Bob LeBaron. He was the morning guy. That other guy worked for some ad agency. I forget his name."

Mrs. Costello's youthful self sported a puffy Farrah Fawcett hairdo with flying buttresses of sprayed hair. Ed, with his arm around her, appeared to be just entering middle age and in denial. He had an over-gelled brown hairdo and wide silver sideburns. The two other women from Sales Support lurched against each other, looking smashed. Bob LeBaron was ogling one of them. Off to the side, next to the anonymous guy from an ad agency, sat a pudgy young man with a wispy mustache wearing a T-shirt that said "The KZZ Fun Guys."

Mrs. Costello tapped his image with a carefully manicured nail. "Ed always felt kind of sorry for Chip. He was always trying to fix him up with girls. Ed liked everyone to be happy." She turned to the policemen. "Does Chip have anything to do with this?"

"We don't know, ma'am," said MacNab. "But we have reason to believe Chip and your husband have been in contact quite recently."

She turned away and scooped up a fluffy white dog that slept on the sofa next to her. It opened one beady little eye, then went back to sleep. She stroked its fur rather desperately. "There's so much Ed didn't tell me." Her masklike features twisted into a face full of pain.

"My guess is he was trying to protect you," said MacNab sympathetically. "Whatever he may have done, no matter how illegal or whatever, I think it was all for you and your security."

She stared down at the photo album. "That was taken at our engagement party. They made me quit. Station policy. You couldn't report to a spouse. But I didn't mind. I was marrying the boss. Sure, he was a little older, but he was so slick. He could get comp tickets to anything. He knew everyone in the media. TV weathermen, everyone."

She sighed. "When I married him, everything looked so rosy. KZZ was making so much money, and Ed was the sales manager. We had a time-share in Hawaii, we went skiing in Colorado. We took the clients to Reno and stuff. Everything was great. It was really glamorous and exciting. It looked like Ed was going to make station manager. Then radio changed. AM was dog meat. Ed ended up with that shitty little job at KLEG."

She sighed fretfully. "Bob LeBaron got him that job. God, Bob's life fell apart too. At KZZ he was really big-time. He went out with stewardesses back when they had to be really cute. He was in celebrity golf tournaments and everything."

She stared at the policeman. "When I met Ed, there was this sweet guy my age who wanted to marry me. He had a job at the post office and he loved kids. Not like Ed, who said he was too old to start a family. If I'd married Dale, I could have had kids. He's a postmaster now. I bet he'll have a pretty decent pension."

"Things always turn out different than you think," said Mac-Nab.

During Lorraine's life review, Lukowski had been staring down at the photo album. The man from the ad agency, the one whose name she had forgotten, looked familiar. Lukowski tried to imagine how he would have aged. When he did that, he recognized him. He'd seen him at the KLEG studios, wearing a frayed tweed jacket and acting as if he didn't really belong there.

"Mrs. Costello," he said, "I'd like to borrow this picture of your engagement party. I'll return it to you."

She waved her hand aggressively in the air. "Keep it. I don't care. My mom told me to grab Dale, but did I listen? No! I was too young and stupid. Instead, I marry Mr. Slick, and he ends up murdered in a Hide-A-Bed at that crappy little station with ratings in the toilet."

Franklin skimmed his latest effort with satisfaction:

To: Phil Bernard, program director
From: Franklin Payne, acting station manager

It has come to my attention that many of the promotional CDs we receive free of charge from record companies have not been unpacked, cataloged or played on the air. I understand this is because of space problems.

To allow new releases to languish in unopened boxes while the shelves are sagging with scratchy old LPs is not acceptable. As far as I'm concerned, most of the old performances that were any good have been remastered, and a lot of them weren't that hot in the first place. I have therefore arranged to sell the record collection to raise some ready money. The dealer will come in over the weekend with spot cash and a hand truck. I will handle the entire transaction. Please have all the LPs (as well as any 78s, wax cylinders or piano rolls you may have squirreled away over the years) boxed up and ready to be removed from the premises by close of business on Friday. Packing containers will be provided.

I'm working on finding a home for the turntables too. Perhaps we can donate them to a school, orphanage or broadcast facility in some developing country that still uses treadle sewing machines and ox-drawn plows.

He sauntered over toward Judy's desk, whistling, and dropped the memo on her desk. "Type this up and make sure Phil gets it," he said.

Judy read the memo and gasped. "Phil will be very upset," she said, growing even paler.

"I'm sorry to hear that," said Franklin in a voice calculated to convey that he wasn't a bit sorry. "I want you to run up to U-Haul on Aurora Avenue and pick up about fifty cardboard boxes and some packing tape." He rubbed his hands together. "Don't you just love throwing out old useless crap? I do." He gave her a meaningful look, but she didn't seem to get that he was referring to her. Oh, well, not every act of terrorism could hit home.

"Speaking of throwing stuff out," he continued, "when you get back can you please clean out the fridge? Something in there seems to be sprouting."

"Those are my lentils," said Judy defensively. "They're suppose to sprout. I was going to have them for lunch."

"Oh. Lunch." Franklin consulted his watch. It was way too early for lunch, but he could use a snack. "Could you pick me up a hamburger on your way back?"

"I'm afraid I can't handle products made from dead animals. I will become physically ill."

"Really?" said Franklin. "You mean throw up and everything? Just from touching a Big Mac? I find that pretty hard to believe."

Judy shut her eyes and seemed to be expressing strong emotion by flexing her closed blue-veined eyelids. The effect she created was rather like a petit mal seizure. "My system is very sensitive. I try not to be judgmental about what others choose to put inside their bodies, but I know that eating meat is criminal." She opened her eyes and said confidently, "I'm convinced that killing an animal in order to eat it will someday be considered murder under our legal system."

"That's ridiculous," snapped Franklin. "Our legal system is based on the Western idea of the sanctity of *human* life, a tradition that is thousands of years old and that has served us well. Do you actually believe wringing some chicken's neck for dinner is the same as murdering poor Ed Costello?"

"Oh, no," said Judy in a calm, kindergarten-teacher voice. "Ed Costello was a human being, capable of evil. People are lower than animals. Animals are innocent. I feel sure that whoever killed Ed probably had very good reason. It may well be that his murder was morally justifiable. Killing a chicken is much worse." She smiled.

Franklin decided she was completely insane. He didn't like the strange gleam in her eyes, or her calm, mad voice. "Yeah, well, skip the burger," he said, backing away. As he did, he caught Alice Jordan's eye. She had apparently overheard their conversation. He didn't think it was his imagination that she rolled her eyes toward the ceiling as if to indicate that she too thought Judy was out of her mind. He felt a rush of warm feeling toward Alice. Unlike everyone else here, she seemed sane. Weepy and neurotic, maybe, but not nuts.

With a lot of heavy sighing, Judy gathered up her big hand-bag—Franklin had hoped it was leather so he could confront her with using animal products, but it seemed to be woven from old creosote-covered ropes—and left the office.

He now felt free to make a phone call without fear of her listening in. Inside Caroline's office, he slid the glass doors closed. He called a radio station broker based in Dallas and asked him how much he thought he could get for a 5,000-watt AM radio station in Seattle.

The broker asked a few questions about the transmitter, the equipment, the signal. "AM only, huh?" he said after a little intake of breath that sounded like a wince. Franklin felt like someone trying to get a car dealer to take a pathetic rusted-out junker as a trade-in. "To tell you the truth," the man in Dallas went on, "we hardly ever deal with those in any kind of decent-sized market unless they're part of a package with some FM station. Most of our deals involve station trades by national players who are taking advantage of relaxed ownership rules in broadcasting, and building station groups in major markets.

"Your best bet is some church. That or an ethnic group that

wants to broadcast in Vietnamese or Spanish or whatever. Basically, a low-wattage AM like that, it's only going to be of interest to someone going after a small niche listenership.

"Still, the dial position and a little equipment, maybe you can get yourself $500,000 for it. That's just a wild guess. Don't hold me to it."

Half a million for unloading this black hole sounded pretty good to Franklin. He wondered if he'd been too hasty, blowing off Chip Gilmore. Unless some Esperanto enthusiasts miraculously appeared with ready cash soon, Chip looked like his best bet. Maybe he could raise a half million dollars from car washes or illegal arms sales.

It would be well worth paying a broker a hefty commission to eat bad food with Chip and Ron Ott in that hideous Italianate restaurant and to deal with the Federal Communications Commission. He'd see if they were still interested. And he'd also make sure they didn't call him here at the station where they would be overheard.

Later, when the on-air ranting about the new world order began, Franklin could tell Caroline he was shocked, shocked, that the broker had come up with buyers who were demented hatemongers. He began to dig through the wastebasket for the Post-it note with Chip's number.

CHAPTER NINETEEN

Lukowski presented himself at the station later that morning to pick up the tape Teresa had promised. "I'm here to see Carl Weeb," he informed Judy.

"May I ask what it's concerning?" she said aggressively.

Lukowski ignored her. "He's back in that record library, I take it," he said, breezing past her desk.

In the record library, Carl looked up from a large cardboard box, nodded silently, then went to his desk and picked a cassette out of a drawer. He handed it to Lukowski.

Also in the room was Phil Bernard, who didn't notice the transaction because his head was down on the desk in front of him, face down on his folded arms. He appeared to be heaving slightly.

Next to him stood Daphne Hamilton, patting him on the back. "It'll be okay, Phil," she was saying. "Really."

"What's the matter?" said Lukowski, startled at the highly charged scene.

Carl shrugged. "Phil's kind of upset."

Phil remained collapsed on the desk, but his head snapped up. Strands of hair hung in front of his flushed face, and his eyes behind his crooked glasses had a wild look in them. "Civilization is dead," he announced to Lukowski. "The barbarians have stormed the gates. They are inside the walls of the city." He let his head fall back down on his folded arms, and Daphne began to rub his back.

"Is he okay?" asked Lukowski.

Carl shrugged. "The boss just told him we're getting rid of all the old LPs." He indicated a cardboard box full of record jackets and unceremoniously threw in a handful more, then pulled some packing tape off a roll with a screechy sound and sealed the box.

"I see. I guess. Is Bob LeBaron around?" asked Lukowski, glancing at the bare dusty shelves where the LPs had sat.

"He'll be in at eleven for a staff meeting," said Daphne, looking up at Lukowski.

Phil Bernard's head popped back up again. "I'm going to make it very clear that we can't go through with this. It's too horrible," he said defiantly. "Carl! Stop that! Put those records back. And in the proper order!"

Carl shrugged. "Franklin told me not to pay any attention to you if you said that." He shoved the full box toward the door with his foot. Lukowski had the idea that in his passive, affectless way, Carl was relishing Phil's pain.

Phil pounded his desk. "We'll all stand up to Franklin. The whole staff will back me up. They have to!" Spittle had formed at the corners of his mouth, giving him the look of a rabid dog.

Lukowski withdrew, reflecting that his own office politics were played out with a lot less drama. And a good thing, too, since where he worked most of the participants were armed. Still, one of the KLEG staff had ended up with a bullet in his chest. Maybe it was time to have a word with that sensible, pleasant Alice Jordan about the high feelings around the place.

As he walked down the darkened corridor back to the main reception area, he heard a whispered "Hey!" behind him. Carl, bent over a box, was pushing his way down the passage.

He straightened up and whispered, "I listened to that tape I made of Ed last night. There's some weird stuff there. Apparently I wasn't the only one Ed was blackmailing."

Lukowski nodded and said noncommittally, "I'll look forward to hearing it."

"And there's another thing," said Carl hurriedly, looking over his shoulder. "It sounds like Bob LeBaron knew about the call-girl operation. Don't tell him I gave you the tape, okay? If he gets into trouble, I don't want him coming after me." Suddenly he jerked his head back and stood like a deer in the forest, listening. Then he yelled, "Daphne! Dead air!"

Daphne came flying down the corridor toward the studio door. Screaming "Jesus Christ," she slammed Lukowski aside, then plunged into the booth. "Ah," said her calm voice from an overhead speaker a second later. "Daphne Hamilton, back with you here on Classic KLEG. I thought a little pregnant pause was in order—a moment to reflect on the stunning beauty of that moving Partita No. 2 in D Major by Johann Sebastian Bach."

In the manager's office, Franklin listened to her and slid out from behind the desk. He'd go down to the record library right now and chew Phil out for letting one of his announcers refer to the station as a horsefly—and use Bach's full name. Franklin's memo on the subject had been very specific.

As he emerged purposefully into the reception area, he noticed Detective Lukowski leaning cozily on the partition to Alice Jordan's cubicle. "If I could just ask you a few general questions," he was saying. "You seem to be a very observant person." Alice was beaming back up at him in a hero-worshiping way that Franklin found irritating.

"Say," he interrupted, "have you people found out who broke in here?"

"As a matter of fact," said Lukowski, "I was going to talk to you both about that. Have either of you had any dealings with a Charles W. Gilmore?"

"No," said Alice, looking disappointed that she couldn't contribute something.

"Why do you ask?" said Franklin evasively.

"Mr. Gilmore was apparently associated with Ed Costello in some way," said Lukowski, as if trying to prod their memories. "He's also apparently involved with some militia-type group."

"Chip!" said Alice triumphantly. She turned to Franklin. "Remember? That Chip character. I called his machine. Could that be the same person?" She looked back at Lukowski. "I found his number among Ed's papers."

Franklin put on a blank face, wishing Chip's name had not come up, but Alice went on. "You told me he was nuts and not to call him again."

"Oh. Yes." Franklin feigned dawning recall. "Chip Gilmore." He turned back to Lukowski. "What does he have to do with this?"

"We found his fingerprints on the glass in the bathroom window."

"On the outside?" said Alice, barely able to contain her excitement.

"That's right."

"Oh!" she said, clasping her hands together with girlish joy.

"Franklin and I figured out what he took too. A catalog of Asian mail-order brides. It's all pretty strange."

Franklin cleared his throat. He certainly wasn't going to discuss the fact that Chip wanted to buy KLEG. Not in front of Alice Jordan. Judy up at the front desk was probably listening with her super hearing to everything, too.

Neither did Franklin want to volunteer the fact that he'd just left messages on Chip's machine and with Ron Ott's adenoidal secretary, asking them in a friendly way if they'd scraped some money together yet. If they had, he'd give them the name of the Dallas broker. "I believe Ed knew this Chip character back at KZZ years ago," he said instead.

Lukowski reached into his jacket and produced the photograph he'd gotten from Lorraine Costello. "That's right," he said. "Here's a picture of Mr. Gilmore with Ed Costello taken some years ago. Recognize him?" Lukowski tapped the face of Chip Gilmore.

Alice peered eagerly at the photograph. "The guy with the round head?" she asked. "Wow. Which one's Ed?"

"The oily-looking character with sideburns pawing the babe," said Franklin, his lip curling.

"That's Mrs. Costello," said Lukowski. "This was taken at their engagement party. I also wondered if you could identify this individual," said Lukowski. "I noticed him here at the station last time I was here."

Franklin squinted at the snapshot. "My God," he said, "that's my sister's latest boyfriend. Jeffrey something. Fleming. He's on the road with Caroline in Arizona. What's he doing there?"

"Isn't that Bob LeBaron, too?" said Alice.

A low baritone voice rumbled across the room. "Did I hear my name?" he said. "Not being taken in vain, I trust."

"We were just looking at a picture of you from your salad days," said Franklin. Bob came over, and Lukowski handed the picture to him.

"Gosh, that brings back some memories," he said. "KZZ. It was what we called an M.O.R. format—middle of the road— before everything in radio got segmented into a lot of mindless demographics. It was personality radio. We'd play music everyone liked, but mostly, people thought of us as warm, personal friends. We used to read all the spots live and an endorsement from a KZZ jock meant something. I'd say I liked a restaurant, everyone would rush over there, hoping to catch a glimpse of me." He sighed. "I never paid for a drink or a meal for years. Everyone knew Bob LeBaron, the top-rated morning man in the market."

Bob allowed his head to lean back, and his face took on a sentimental glow. He seemed to be preparing to share more happy memories, so Franklin snapped, "Yeah, I know. The expense account was bottomless and you all hung out at Trader Vic's drinking cocktails with paper umbrellas and gardenias in them."

"You recognize any of these folks?" said Lukowski, shoving the snapshot at Bob.

Bob fished a pair of dingy reading glasses from a plastic holder in his shirt pocket. "Let's see. There's Ed and his wife. A couple of gals from the sales department. Wendy was always a lot of fun. Couldn't hold her liquor, but that was okay too," he said with a leer. "Poor little Chip. And some guy from an ad agency. Kind of a crony of Ed's for a while. I forget his name. They had some scam going. Ed always had a scam going, bless him."

"Why did you say 'poor little Chip'?" asked Alice.

Bob chuckled. "Well, surrounded by a bunch of highfliers

such as myself, he felt a little out of it. Every time we went into Trader Vic's, Ed would turn bright red and get all excited when this little Chinese gal—Michiko was her name—would flutter all over us."

"Yeah, yeah," said Franklin impatiently. "Orchid over her left ear. But Michiko is a Japanese name."

"Well, she was some kind of Oriental. Cute as a button. Anyway, we'd let little Chip tag along sometimes. Kind of our mascot. I'd fool around on the air, teasing him, you know. I'd get a lot of mileage out of him. I'd say stuff like 'Our engineer, Chip, the lonely bachelor, looks like he finally had a wild night last night.' People started writing him fan letters. Anyway, we'd go into Trader Vic's and he had the hots for this Michiko. So anyway . . ."

Franklin shifted his weight from one foot to the other and reminded himself that with the exception of the upcoming staff meeting, Bob was safely exiled to the six to midnight shift where there was no one for him to bore except the radio audience.

Bob rattled on. "Ed was always the kind of guy who liked to get everyone fixed up, you know?"

"The vice squad knows that now," said Franklin.

"Yeah, well, he told Chip he could get him a sweet little Oriental wife who'd give him back rubs and bring him his slippers."

"Really?" said Alice.

"Yeah. And damned if he didn't. Six weeks later, Chip was engaged to some little lotus blossom."

Franklin toyed briefly with the idea of firing Bob LeBaron on the spot on the grounds of racial and gender insensitivity. Let him sue for age discrimination then.

Bob raised an eyebrow rakishly and seemed about to nudge Lukowski in the ribs with an elbow. "We gave him a stag party you wouldn't believe. Got a lot of on-air mileage from that. You better believe it. We skated pretty near the edge on the air. People tuned in just to find out if we'd go over the edge, you know. It was always in good taste, though. Risqué but tasteful."

"Did Ed find a wife for Chip in one of those mail-order bride catalogs?" asked Alice.

"He sure did," said Bob with a chuckle. "Wrote her some cornball letters and stuck Chip's picture in the mail. Before we knew it, she was over here and they hit it off. At first, anyway. I heard later the whole thing fizzled out and she went back to Hong Kong or wherever she came from. But at least Chip got himself a honeymoon. Good old Ed."

Caroline drifted out onto the balcony overlooking the immaculate green lawn around the pool. Beyond thick adobe walls was desert with dramatic saguaro cactuses, and in the distance lay brown hills drenched with a rosy sunset.

She carried a margarita and wore a long, sheer white cotton gauze garment, accented by the huge turquoise-and-silver squash-blossom necklace and matching drop earrings she'd just bought in the lobby gift store.

"Darling," she said, "come out here and smell the mesquite. It's divine."

Jeffrey Fleming came outside. He carried a camera with a telephoto lens and wore white linen trousers and the loose, pale blue Mexican shirt Caroline had just bought for him in the same gift store because it matched his eyes.

Below them, immobile hotel guests in loud shorts and sundresses exposing abundant pale flesh sat sprawled around the patio. Slim, dark, fully clothed Hispanics moved elegantly and quickly among them, bringing drinks and plates of food. Bra-

162

ziers around the perimeter took the desert chill from the air and provided the tang of mesquite.

"Oh, darling," said Caroline. "It's lovely here, I know, but so depressingly bourgeois after our week in the trailer parks. Maybe we did the wrong thing."

"No, no!" said Jeffrey eagerly. He squinted down at the patio through his camera. "There's great stuff here. I'm thinking it's time for me to move on, creatively speaking. Look at those big white toads sitting around down there. They all look so miserable! I can see a whole show just devoted to assholes in luxury resorts. I could do this for months!"

He turned to her. "I think I've taken the trailer-trash thing as far as I can. It's time for a complete change of direction." He leaned over and kissed her. "Darling, you've inspired me! I'm looking at everything with fresh eyes."

"Sweetheart," she said, nuzzling his neck with the top of her head, "it is wonderful, isn't it? Seattle and KLEG seem so far away."

"Forget about KLEG," he said. "Let's just keep going. From resort to resort, golf course to golf course. I can do some great stuff with pools and tennis courts, too."

She turned away from him. "I feel so guilty, Jeffrey. I have a responsibility to carry on Mother's work at KLEG. Franklin wants us to sell it, just because it loses money every month."

"It loses money every month?" said Jeffrey. "Really?"

"Well, you—an artist, of all people—know how unimportant money is," she said airily.

"Of course I do. But I'm so selfish, darling, and so in love. I want all your attention. And I want to stay on the road with you forever. I can really see this resort thing developing into a great coffee-table book." He gazed out into the desert. "There's so much here for me creatively. The opulence and then the desert as a metaphor for, like, a desert kind of thing. You know?"

"Oh, Jeffrey, I know exactly," she said. "Maybe I should just follow my heart and turn my back on my life's work with KLEG."

"I don't want to tell you what to do, Caroline," he said earnestly, "but if that thing's losing money, I'd drop it like a bad habit."

CHAPTER TWENTY

Franklin was winding up his speech to the troops at the KLEG staff meeting. "And in conclusion, I'd encourage you all to think about ways you could seek new career challenges elsewhere. I'm not sure what the future of KLEG will be. It would be irresponsible of me to encourage any of you to count on KLEG for the long term.

"My sister and I cannot continue to run the station as a public service. Anyway, the fact that very few members of the public bother to tune in indicates that the service we are providing isn't something the public wants."

"So what are you saying, exactly?" said Bob LeBaron with a puzzled frown.

"I'm saying that there's a chance this place is going down the tubes, and so will you if you don't find something else to do with your lives," said Franklin. He gazed out at their pale, startled faces. "If a suitable buyer can be found . . ." He trailed off. Maybe they could get jobs as Wal-Mart greeters.

"But that's not fair!" said Judy.

"What can we do to keep KLEG going just like it is, but better?" asked Daphne. "There must be *something* we can do."

"Well, if you win the lottery, I'll sell you the place for half a million bucks," said Franklin. "Until then we can all work hard to keep overhead down, increase revenues and improve the quality of our on-air product so that Alice will have something decent to sell."

"Our on-air product suffered a disastrous blow today," said Phil with a catch in his voice. "To see our fine archive of fabulous vinyl LPs boxed up and—"

"We've already discussed that," said Franklin sharply. "Let's not get spastic over plastic. Just forget about it."

Phil made a whimpering sound, like an injured animal, but everyone ignored him.

"You don't understand," said Judy in a shrill voice. "You have to put more money into this place if you want it to succeed."

"Yes," said Daphne enthusiastically. "You should be promoting the station on TV, on billboards all over town. Hiring PR firms to plug the on-air personalities. Getting the word out. Making it sound fun and exciting!"

"Daphne's right," Bob LeBaron chimed in. "Back at KZZ we had a crack promotion department. Gosh, they came up with fabulous contests. People were winning cruises and cars. Why, there was even a Date with Bob contest." He chuckled. "This is a great story. You see, there was this little gal who entered about a million times—"

Franklin cut him off. "You people are living in a dream world," he said in an exasperated voice. "I'm trying to do the decent thing and let you know how things stand. Okay, don't believe me if you don't want to. But don't say I didn't warn you."

No one seemed to hear him, but they were all animated and attentive when Judy piped up: "We're not going to give up without a fight. With our talent and commitment, there's no way we can just disappear. We're an institution."

"You all belong in one," Franklin muttered under his breath.

"We need KLEG T-shirts and bumper stickers," Daphne said bouncily. "Let's plan a whole PR campaign!"

"Fine," said Franklin, throwing up his hands. "You can finance it with a bake sale. I'm going to work now. I have a real job in the real world."

Alice Jordan rose and said something in a subdued voice about making some sales calls. The rest of them sat there nattering away like a bunch of kids in a 1940s musical, planning to put together a fabulous show in the old barn. The exception was Carl, who, as usual, sat silent and depressed-looking. He rose obediently when Judy snapped, "Get the phone, Carl."

In the parking lot, Franklin saw Alice getting into her car. She looked just as crushed as she had that day she'd come dragging in after losing the Carlson's Clock Shop sponsorship.

"Listen," he said gruffly, "I'm sorry I sounded so negative. I just thought everyone needed a reality check. I do want to tell you you've been showing real spirit and hustle out there."

She smiled weakly. "Thank you," she said. "And I appreciate your honesty about KLEG's future. It's just that I've been through a kind of unstable time, and to be brutally frank, no one but Caroline wanted to hire me and—" Her eyes pooled up with tears. "I just feel kind of fragile. I'm sorry."

"Don't cry!" he said with alarm.

"I'm sorry," she repeated, blinking furiously. "I've always cried easily, ever since I was a little kid. It's so humiliating. I must just have bigger tear ducts than other people or something." A big teardrop rolled down her cheek, and she wiped it away with the back of her hand. "I just got anxious, thinking I'll be out of a job again so soon after trying so hard to get one, and I've got a kid to support all by myself."

"What about the kid's father?" said Franklin. "Where's he? What does he do?" Franklin found himself suddenly irate at whatever cad could have left this poor helpless, weeping woman to raise his child by herself.

"My husband—well, ex-husband, I mean—is a dentist."

"A dentist? And you can't get any child support out of him?" Franklin found this hard to believe.

Now Alice burst into a sob. "It's all so humiliating. He just abandoned his practice and ran off with Marilyn, his hygienist. Before I knew what he'd done, he managed to turn over most of our joint assets to Marilyn's guru."

"What?"

"It's this woman named Marina who runs a community in northern California and channels the spirits of dolphins and other aquatic mammals."

"That's ridiculous," said Franklin. Years of Caroline's irrational fiscal behavior made him sympathetic to anyone saddled with an irresponsible family member. "He can't transfer community property like that. And besides, he can't just bail out of child support. He must have some current income you can get your hands on."

"He and Marilyn live there, cleaning and filling the teeth of communards for free while the dolphin lady flies around the country in her own Cessna."

"You need a good lawyer," said Franklin sharply.

"I have a legal aid lawyer," said Alice. "But since the Republicans are cutting legal aid for civil things—" Alice looked frazzled. "Oh. But maybe you're a Republican," she said.

"Some of my best friends are Republicans," said Franklin

with a smile. "But my parents made sure I could never be one without seeming ridiculous."

"Really?" said Alice. Her eyes dried up and widened with curiosity. "How did they do that?"

"I don't tell everyone this," he said. "But if you promise not to reveal my secret, I'll tell you. My middle initial is D., and it stands for Delano."

"Oh," said Alice. "Franklin Delano Payne. That's sweet." She giggled.

He giggled back. Hearing about her humiliation at the hands of that stupid dentist and the dolphin-channeling charlatan, Franklin had been seized with the desire to confide to her some little thing about himself. Suddenly he realized that he was having this rather piquant conversation standing up in the middle of the oily and trash-strewn gravel parking lot outside the studios of the hated KLEG. He had a sudden urge to take Alice somewhere pleasant and cheer her up.

"What are you doing for lunch?" he said.

She held up a brown lunch bag. "I was going to eat this in a park," she said. "It's sort of nice to get away from the station."

"I can believe that," said Franklin, shuddering at the thought of that break room with the mean-eyed Judy and the grungy Carl rustling their paper bags in unison. "Come with me. We'll go somewhere nice."

"Oh," she said, "I can't. I promised I'd meet with Detective Lukowski. He's bringing his lunch and meeting me in the park." She turned pink. "Strictly business, of course. I guess because I inherited Ed's job he thought I might have some insights into the case."

Franklin was surprised at his feeling of disappointment. "Another time, then," he said curtly and went over to his own car.

He recalled how the detective had been hanging in that familiar way over her cubicle partition and turning on the charm. An angry feeling of territoriality came over him, and he thought, How dare a public servant hit on my employees like that, right there in front of me at my own radio station.

Alice Jordan was clearly a vulnerable woman. Spirited and brave in her own way, but essentially helpless, bursting into tears all the time. She'd already let that half-witted dentist and his floozy hygienist roll right over her. Now that predatory cop was coming on to her. Clearly, one of life's victims.

He sighed and slid behind the wheel. He mustn't let himself get worked up about the character flaws of all the lame ducks at KLEG. They would all have to make their own way in the world and let him get on with his life.

As Franklin turned the key in the ignition, Phil's voice came out of the speakers. "I can be silent no longer."

"Oh, yes you can," said Franklin through clenched teeth. He rummaged in a nest of tapes at his side and jammed one into the machine, replacing Phil's peevish tones with a Brahms piano trio. So what if Chip Gilmore had broken the bathroom window at KLEG and let himself in? If the little worm could come up with the scratch, Franklin would sell him the station and try to get the deal done before Caroline came back.

Daphne Hamilton stared in horror through the glass into the studio. She was on shift, and she'd drifted out during the Berlioz *Symphonie Fantastique*—sixty-seven minutes, to run across the street to the convenience store for some kitty litter and Pond's dry skin cream. She'd come back with fifteen minutes to spare, but Phil was in the booth, talking. Had she somehow miscalculated? Was her watch wrong? Had there been dead air once again, and had Phil rushed in to save her?

Slowly it dawned on her that Phil sounded peculiar. "For too long now," he was saying in a lugubrious tone, "I have been silent about certain practices here at the station. I went along like a good soldier, simply obeying orders. But there are times when conscience dictates another course. I must tell all of my radio friends, loyal listeners who have been with me for lo these many years, about a grave injustice perpetrated by the management of this venerable radio station—KLEG, a Seattle institution that has fallen on hard times, musically, ethically, morally."

Daphne listened in horror, and Carl and Judy came up beside her as Phil rolled on.

"Today I was told by Franklin Payne, the owner of KLEG, to remove our wonderful collection of LPs from the record library. Our long-playing records of these fabulous performances, great music played by sensitive musicians, are being sold, sent down the river, the collection to be scattered to the four winds. It brings to mind, does it not, the destruction of the library at Alexandria?"

Suddenly Phil's voice took on a grim determination. "But I have news for the barbarians. They can consign a proud heritage to the flames with their scorched-earth policy, but their flames of destruction cannot consume the dwindling embers of culture, because when the smoke clears, they will have surely burned their bridges."

"Wow," said Carl.

"He just broke in to the Berlioz," said Judy. "I can't believe it."

Bob LeBaron, who had been hanging around the station bothering people with his complaints about KLEG and his reminiscences about KZZ ever since the staff meeting had broken up, emerged from the bathroom and joined the others outside the studio window. "What's Phil doing?" he said.

"Mixing metaphors," said Carl.

"Poor Phil," murmured Daphne. "I never realized how far gone he was. Oh, the hurt that man has!"

Phil turned toward the row of shocked faces pressed against the glass and gave them a mad grin, then stuck out his tongue and waggled his hands at them. He turned back to the mike and continued in somber tones. "In what I hope will be perceived as a noble gesture, although perhaps, sadly, a farewell gesture, I'm going to stay here as long as I can and keep the flame of civilization alive. I've locked myself in the booth with several cartons of LPs. I will play them for you, commercial free, for as long as I can. The last sounds you hear will no doubt be those of the scuffle as I am carted off by the forces of darkness. Listen to the dying tones, the Götterdämmerung, of a golden age. The lights are going out all over Seattle. They may not be lit again in our lifetime."

"He's seriously disturbed," said Judy. "We have to take control. Let's run in and overpower him. Bob, you can grab the microphone and say something about Phil being indisposed, then go right back into the Berlioz."

Bob LeBaron seemed not to hear. "Gosh," he said. "The old announcer-locking-himself-in-the-booth gimmick. That's a classic. Often combined with the one-record gimmick. I remember it the first time back at that little station in Walla Walla where I started out. We had this fellow go in there and play 'Rockin' Robin' six hundred and twenty times, screaming and whooping in between. It was the talk of the county for months. Boy, that got their attention. It was in all the papers."

"I say we just let him carry on," said Carl quietly. "We've been covering for him for too long."

Bob chuckled. "Back at KZZ we pulled that locked-booth thing every once in a while during a rating period. We had sound-effects tapes of people busting through the door with an ax, breaking glass, the whole bit. Play-by-play of men in white coats strapping the guy into a straitjacket. It was a real kick. TV stations came down and got footage of our guys bouncing off the glass. It was fabulous publicity."

Judy clenched her jaw in a determined way. "We'll be a laughingstock. We have to go in there and stop him." She rattled the door handle. "He wasn't kidding. It is locked," she announced.

Carl shrugged. "He said he was going to play some of those old LPs. Wait until he's into some music or you'll hand him that audible scuffle he promised his listeners, and you'll make a big martyr of him."

From the reception area they heard the sound of ringing phones.

"We could shut down the transmitter," said Judy.

"Let him rant," said Carl. "Who cares? Franklin says this place is doomed anyway."

"Maybe Bob is right," said Daphne. "Maybe the press will cover this. Maybe that's the press on those phones now, like when Ed's body was discovered. Maybe TV camera crews will come down here."

Both women instinctively patted their hair into place, as if preparing for the coverage. "Carl, maybe you better help me with the phones," said Judy, hustling off.

Carl ignored her.

"And so," Phil went on, "we begin with the incomparable Glenn Gould, in this 1955 recording of Bach's Goldberg Variations. A misunderstood artist expressing himself musically in a now-maligned medium—the long-playing record. You won't hear a performance like this again." Phil cued up the LP, giving it a little turn so it would have time to get up to speed, then pushed the turntable button.

As the record spun, he sat hunched in his chair, his head turned sideways like a big owl, apparently mesmerized by the sight of the needle traveling across the surface of the record.

Judy came back, panting. "A bunch of listeners want to know what's going on. They think it's weird. Oh! He's into the record now. Let's get him out of there!"

"Why?" asked Carl.

"Because he's out of control," said Judy harshly, rattling the knob again and pounding her fist on the glass.

"You're really into control issues, aren't you, Judy?" said Carl snippily.

Phil pulled himself away from the sight of needle meeting groove and made a kissy face at Judy through the window. She clicked her tongue and rushed out into the reception area.

Daphne said, "We definitely should call the media. Maybe we could get some PR out of this. It would draw attention to the station."

"I don't know," said Bob LeBaron thoughtfully. "That gimmick's pretty old. It would probably have to be a pretty slow news day. They covered it at KZZ because we were already famous. Big personalities around town. Household names. Anyway, everyone knows it's fake."

"I don't think so," said Carl thoughtfully. "Look at him."

Phil was now pacing around the booth, stopping occasionally to throw back his head and laugh wildly. The maniacal sound that came from his mouth, however, could only be imagined, as the glass was soundproof.

Judy rushed back with a piece of typing paper with a crudely lettered felt-tip pen message scrawled on it with apparent haste: "You Must Open the Door. Now!" Assuming a fierce expression, she plastered her sign against the glass.

Phil stopped pacing, made an exaggerated bow and waggled his index finger from side to side, then executed a few stiff dance steps.

"He looks like old Dr. Drosselmeyer in *The Nutcracker*," said Carl.

Judy produced a second piece of paper with a second message: "We'll have to come in and get you."

Phil straightened up, closed his eyes and shook his head from side to side like a stubborn toddler, then began pushing big boxes of LPs up against the door.

"A screwdriver," said Judy. "I bet we can get in there with a screwdriver."

"The toolbox is inside the booth," said Carl.

"Maybe I've got something in my car we can use," said Judy, dashing off again.

"We must call the media," said Daphne decisively. "Any publicity is good publicity. We can explain how the Paynes want to sell the station. Maybe there will be a public outcry."

"I suppose I could call my old friend Rex Blaine," said Bob LeBaron.

"God, Rex Blaine," said Carl with a moan. "Is he still on TV? He did the news when I was a little kid. He had weird hair with too much Brylcreem in it."

Bob looked a little miffed. "Hey, he was the market's number one TV anchor when I was the number one radio morning man. Okay, so maybe he's not anchoring anymore since they demoted all the mature white guys, but he had a lifetime contract with that TV station, and he wouldn't let them buy him out. They've got him doing soft features until he retires at seventy."

"Oh, yeah," said Daphne. She turned to Carl and explained. "*Blaine's Byways.* He travels around the state in an old VW van with a poodle, looking for oddball feature stories. You know, houses made of old bottle caps and greased-pig contests at county fairs."

Bob chuckled. "I'll call Rex and tell him this stunt of Phil's is probably the only known example of the crazed-announcer-locking-himself-in-the-booth gimmick that could be for real."

"Life imitates art," said Daphne. "I like it."

CHAPTER TWENTY-ONE

While the KLEG staff had held its meeting, Lukowski had left the station and returned to his office. He and MacNab had sat and listened to Ed Costello's tape. Afterward they looked at each other. "A thousand bucks. Is that worth killing someone over?" asked MacNab.

"If you thought it might not be a onetime-only payment," answered MacNab. "Anyway, it'll take the forensics guys about ten minutes to work out from those phone blips just whose number he was calling, and we can check it out."

By the time Lukowski was ready to leave for his park-bench lunch date with Alice Jordan, they had their answer. The number Ed Costello had called, before apparently successfully blackmailing someone, had been Jeffrey Fleming's number.

"Interesting," said Lukowski. "He's Caroline Payne's new boyfriend. I saw him down at the station earlier. And he was also in that picture Mrs. Costello gave us. Franklin Payne said he and Caroline were on the road. Arizona, I think."

"I'll find out what I can about him while you're gone," said MacNab. "Maybe this will finally start making some sense."

*   *   *

Back at his law offices, Franklin's secretary told him that Ron Ott was on line three. Franklin decided to play dumb about the break-in and see if Chip was still in the market for KLEG. Let him buy it and he could fix the broken bathroom window himself.

"Listen, Ron," said Franklin, "I just wanted you to know that there is some interest from another quarter in buying KLEG. Seeing as we had already spoken, I thought it only fair to let you know." In a move inspired to motivate Chip to get his cash together for ideological reasons, he added, "It's an ethnic, multicultural thing. These folks want to use the station to broadcast in a lot of Third World languages."

"I see," said Ott. "I suggest we meet once again, over at Mr. Gilmore's house. He's decided to be more forthcoming about his possible funding source."

"Well," said Franklin, "I'm not sure I can help him there. I mean—"

"I know it's a little irregular, but"—here Ott took on a collegial manner that Franklin found insulting—"let's face it, some clients are a little irregular. Just a little whimsical. Still, I think if you put it to him there's another buyer, maybe you can help him pull a deal together, because of specialized knowledge you might have based on Mr. Costello's efforts."

"I don't know what the hell you're talking about, Mr. Ott," said Franklin, who decided to drop the friendly "Ron."

"All will become clear in due course," said Ott with smug mysteriousness. "I want you to hear Mr. Gilmore's story from his own lips."

"Oh, all right," said Franklin. Who knew when Caroline would reappear to muddy the waters? Time was of the essence.

Franklin agreed to let Ott come by the office later that afternoon and take him to Chip's house.

Lukowski sat on a park bench between Alice and the bag containing his Taco Bell lunch. He was turning his head to accom-
modate a messy beef burrito and listening to her talk while she
peeled and separated a navel orange and placed the sections in a
neat row on the napkin in her lap.

"To be honest," she said, "I've given it a lot of thought. Being
new and all, there's not a lot I know, but I've been listening and
watching."

"Excellent," said Lukowski. "What do you hear about Caroline Payne's boyfriend, Jeffrey Fleming?"

"Is that his name? All I know is that Judy, who eavesdrops on
everyone's phone conversations, says he's younger and a gigolo
type and probably after Caroline's money. They seem to think
that's her pattern."

"Really? This Judy is spying on everyone?"

"KLEG is a hotbed of high feeling and intrigue," she said.
"Basically, the staff is all paranoid because they're afraid the
owners want to sell the station. Which they do—at least
Franklin does—because it's losing money. I think the employees
have developed a siege mentality. They all seem to think that Ed
was too cozy with management." She leaned forward. "I did hear
that Ed had tried to get Phil Bernard fired."

"Phil Bernard?" said Lukowski.

"The program director. He's been there a million years, and
KLEG is his life. Sometimes he loses it on the air. Ed was taping him to document his outbursts and get him fired."

"You mean the old guy who works in the library?" said

Lukowski. "I saw him in tears today. He seems kind of high-strung."

"They're all kind of high-strung. Judy, the receptionist, for instance. She's said a few things that sound irrational. Like that Ed's murder was probably justifiable homicide. She thinks animals deserve a higher standard of legal protection."

"I see."

"At one point," Alice went on, "she told me not to snitch to management. 'Remember what happened to Ed,' she said. She's really pretty far gone."

"Hmm," said Lukowski. "Doesn't sound like a fun place to work."

"Well, I was a housewife for a long time," Alice said defensively. "I hadn't worked outside the home for many years. I had to take what I could get."

He glanced down at her bare ring finger, half expecting to hear some autobiographical stuff about how she came to be single. Instead, she went on talking about his case.

"But what I think is more intriguing than all those disgruntled employees is that break-in. If Chip Gilmore is some kind of white supremacist type, maybe he doesn't want anyone to know he was once married to an Asian woman. Why else would he come in and steal that catalog? I wonder why Ed had his phone number."

"You said you called it," said Lukowski.

"That's right. I thought it might be someone who wanted to buy advertising. There were dollar signs after the name."

Her eyes widened suddenly. "Wow! Do you think Ed Costello was blackmailing this Chip person? I mean if someone is unscrupulous enough to run a vice ring, maybe he would stoop to blackmail, too. Maybe that's what the dollar signs were there for!"

She started bouncing a little on the park bench, and her cheeks turned a fetching pink. "Maybe Chip killed Ed because he was about to reveal that secret! I mean these nutcases are pretty unhinged—even more so than the KLEG staff, don't you think? And they're into guns. Ed was killed with a gun. What kind was it? Some huge-caliber weapon? That's what Chip would use, I bet."

Lukowski found the scenario she was creating interesting. In fact, Ed Costello had been killed with a great big Glock.

Back at the office, MacNab bustled up to him, flapping papers. "I got the background on this Fleming guy. Apparently he was busted about fifteen years back for some porn shots he took. One of the girls was seventeen. I talked to one of the prosecutors on the case.

"Fleming tried to say it was art, but the jury took a look at the stuff and exercised its own artistic judgment. He also said he was just doing a job for a buddy of his, and the buddy provided the girls. Some female gymnastics team, apparently. Guess who the buddy was."

"Ed Costello?"

"Bingo."

"Interesting. Did he make it stick to Costello?"

"Nope. Costello left him hanging out a mile. Fleming did some community service. An ad agency he was working for fired him."

"And now he's after Caroline Payne's money, according to the employees," said Lukowski. "I also think it's time to go have a chat with Chip Gilmore. It turns out he was once married to one of those Asian women like in the catalog. All set up, incidentally, by good old Ed Costello."

"No kidding," said MacNab.

Lukowski winced. "I hope we're not talking about another Ruby Ridge or Waco. Maybe we better take some extra guys with us. You think he's nuts enough to meet us at the door with some firepower?"

"I don't think so. I talked to the guy that busted him for that parking-lot fight over at the cable station. Basically, he's got a little sleazeball lawyer he calls whenever he gets in trouble. If he sees eight cars pulling up with sirens he might get agitated. I think we'd be safer just knocking on the door."

"Let's see if he's got a Glock pistol lying around that matches the one that killed Costello," said Lukowski.

"God, that'd be pretty convenient," said MacNab. "What kind of motive would he have for taking out Costello?"

"Alice Jordan from the radio station came up with one that's just crazy enough to make sense," said Lukowski. "Where's our copy of the Asian brides catalog the little jerk stole?"

MacNab produced it. The quality of the Xerox copies wasn't great, but on the back cover was a group of wedding shots under the headline "These Lucky Guys Found Lovely Oriental Brides in Our Pages—You Can Too!" One of them, a round-headed man, appeared to be Chip Gilmore in younger days. He wore a wide-lapelled suit and had his arm around a demure little woman in a wedding dress and lace veil who came up to about his shoulder.

"Hey, I've still got the old touch," said Bob LeBaron, ambling back to the glass window. Carl and Daphne were watching in horror as Phil, wielding a hammer from the toolbox, proceeded to dismantle some shelving. Meanwhile, at the studio door, Judy was trying to dislodge the hinges with a jack handle.

"Rex and his canine mascot, Fluffy, are on their way," Bob announced.

Daphne clapped her hands together and said, "Fabulous!"

"First," continued Bob, "they've got to cover an oyster-shucking contest over in Ballard. Rex will call back in about an hour to see if Phil's still in there."

Carl pointed into the booth. "I think he will be. Look. It's just like a Road Runner cartoon." Phil was methodically nailing a two-by-four, stripped from the shelving, across the door and had two more propped up, ready to go.

"Great stuff," said Bob, nodding sagely. "Rex will love it."

"Seeing as I don't think he'll be out of there anytime soon," said Carl, yawning, "I'm giving myself an extra long lunch. In fact, I might take the rest of the day off. God knows, after working for Phil all these years, I deserve it."

"Can't you stick around and help with the phones?" demanded Judy, pausing in her efforts with the jack handle.

Carl shrugged and picked up a line on his way out.

"KLEG, good afternoon," he said. "Oh, hi, Alice. Just a sec." He went over to her desk and spent some time at the Rolodex. "No, it's not here," he said. "Definitely not. Okay. By the way, are you listening to the station? Phil locked himself in the booth and he's having an on-air psychotic break."

At a phone booth near the park where she'd spent longer than she had intended with Detective Lukowski, Alice gasped. She'd wanted to call Rosa Delgado to tell her she might be a few minutes late to pick up the tape, but as always, only the Yellow Pages hung from the shelf in the booth.

Her initial surprise at hearing Rosa Delgado's Rolodex card wasn't there was superseded by her horror at the idea of Phil cracking up on the air. This wouldn't make it any easier to sell time, that was for sure, she thought irritably as she went back to her car.

Although she'd originally thought Ed Costello was out of line trying to establish dominance over the programming staff, now she understood perfectly why he'd wanted to get Phil out of the picture.

In the car she turned on the radio. Phil was saying, "Remember, we're running our reluctant farewell to the long-playing record completely commercial-free. In fact, I've torn up the log with all the ads on it. They were vulgar, horrible things anyway. I've always felt KLEG should operate for the public good, without these crude commercial pitches from advertisers. They just get in the way.

"This is your announcer, Phil Bernard, behind lock and key, barricaded in the studio, bringing you the last gasp of civilization. We'll get into the Hollywood String Quartet's legendary 1958 release of Beethoven's Opus 127 right after this announcement."

Announcement? Maybe he *was* going into a commercial after all. Maybe he'd just been kidding. But no, now he was saying, "This station is conducting a test of the Emergency Broadcast System. This is only a test." A harsh electronic tone came on. Angrily, she turned down the volume.

She could expect immediate and justifiable cancellation from any advertiser who'd happened to hear Phil's tirade. As soon as she picked up the tape from Rosa Delgado, she would call Franklin and demand he fire Phil. The man was obviously out of his mind.

She tried to pull herself together in the elevator. Above all, she must not let Phil Bernard's antics make her eyes pool up with tears. She couldn't let the formidable Rosa Delgado see her all frazzled. Not only was Alice determined to keep this account on the air, she also wanted Rosa to give her a real job—and soon.

Back at his apartment, Carl hummed happily as he flipped through the racks of dresses in Teresa's closet. The red polka-dot rayon number with the short sleeves, he thought. It was a kind of flouncy Betty Grable thing, just brushing the knee. She'd wear it with the black patent pumps with Daisy Duck bows and the big *I Love Lucy* pearl choker and matching earrings.

Lukowski and MacNab stood on the sagging plywood porch of Chip Gilmore's dingy yellow stucco box of a house, and Lukowski knocked his friendly signature knock. Marks on the door suggested that some large animal asking to be let in had removed most of the paint from the bottom half.

The neighborhood had once been full of cute little surburban newlywed houses bought with G.I. loans after World War II. It was now a slummy suburb with the little boxes in various stages of dilapidation or held together with cheap aluminum siding, chain-link fenced yards and listing carports sheltering dead cars and the dregs of pathetic garage sales.

From behind the door came loud barking, the scrabbling noise of claws on floor and a snuffling sound as one or more large dogs pressed noses to the cracks around the door and inhaled the scent of interlopers.

"God," said MacNab, "I remember in my patrol days there was a motorcycle gang lived on this block. We were out here every Saturday night. And notice the Christmas lights? There's three Christmas-lights houses on this one block alone." He shook his head sadly. It was one of his axioms that people who left Christmas lights on year-round were capable of anything. If there was a domestic-violence or child-abuse call and one house on the block still had Christmas lights tacked onto the eaves in August, that was invariably where the call was.

Lukowski knocked again and tried not to think of the dogs tearing out his throat.

"Some people have no pride," MacNab went on, gesturing up and down the block at various ratty front yards. "How much would it cost these folks to mow the lawn? Or paint the god-damn trim? Even if you can't afford to paint the whole house, just touching up the trim makes a big difference."

A young male voice from behind the door yelled, "Fritz, Hans, shut up!" The barking ceased. "Who is it?" demanded the voice.

"Seattle police officers. Just want to ask you a few questions," said MacNab in an amiable tone.

"Not interested. We're not opening this door for no agents of no illegitimately constituted so-called government body."

"Are you Mr. Gilmore?" persisted MacNab. "Maybe you'd like to step outside for a quick word."

"You want to talk to anyone from this house, you talk to our attorney, Ron Ott. He's in the phone book."

"Jesus," muttered MacNab as they left the porch. "Ron Ott. I've had dealings with that little slimeball. I can't believe he hasn't been disbarred yet."

Lukowski looked over his shoulder. Two skinny guys in their twenties with buzz cuts, jeans and bare, pale, underdeveloped torsos were staring at them out the window with stupid yet somehow worried expressions, while a couple of Dobermans slobbered on the window. "Hey, MacNab," he said, "you get the feeling those bald geeks are named Fritz and Hans and we were talking to one of the dogs?"

CHAPTER TWENTY-TWO

Alice had been afraid the tape would simply be sitting at the reception desk with her name on it and she wouldn't get a chance to try to impress Rosa Delgado. Fortunately, Rosa, wearing a tiny but expensive turquoise suit and masses of pearls around her neck, came out to greet her. "Coffee," she said in a gruff tone that sounded more like a command than an offer.

"Yes, thank you," said Alice. Rosa gestured imperiously to the receptionist, who scrambled away.

"Come in. Sit down," said Rosa as she made the long hike around her huge desk to reach the chair. "Sell anything else?"

"Yes," said Alice. "And I want to thank you for the tips you gave me last time I was here. They gave me more confidence." She took in her breath. "In fact, I think I probably have what it takes to be very successful in sales. I mention this because you said last time that you might have openings here."

"That's right. I like you. You have an honest face," said Rosa. "I'm never wrong about anyone. I can tell you're a hard worker, too. Fill out an application. I'll teach you how to sell anything to anybody."

The receptionist appeared with two cups of coffee and gave

Alice a friendly smile. "Get out an application form," Rosa said to her. "Alice will fill it in on her way out."

"Certainly," said the receptionist cheerfully.

What a contrast to the surly Judy, thought Alice. And how different the slightly alarming yet wonderfully decisive Rosa was from the dithery, vague, maddening Caroline Payne Parker.

"How are things at the radio station?" asked Rosa. Alice felt guilty not telling her about Phil's on-air antics, especially as Rosa had just said how honest she was, but Rosa didn't seem to require an answer. "Anyone find out what happened to Ed Costello?"

"Not that I know of," said Alice. "I'm afraid the police don't confide in us." Then, eager to please Rosa, she added, "We did have someone break into the station, though. Looking through Ed's papers."

"Really?"

"Yes," said Alice. "But they know who it is. Someone Ed worked with years ago." It was hard to tell from her brusque demeanor how interested Rosa was. Alice sipped the last of her coffee nervously. Maybe she was boring Rosa, who had said before that she never read crime news. Maybe to go on would reveal Alice's Nancy Drew–like fascination with criminal matters and make her seem ditzy.

Alice fell silent and decided she'd done the right thing, because Rosa didn't ask any more questions about Ed Costello. Instead, she handed Alice a box containing the tape. "There are three commercials here," she said. "Please rotate all the spots equally."

Alice rose. "Yes, of course. Thank you," and then forced herself to show she was an apt pupil by adding, "I'm sure this schedule will provide you with plenty of good leads." Rosa had said the buyer should always be reassured after the sale.

"Maybe you can follow up on some of them," said Rosa with a little smile. "Fill out that application and I'll let you know this week."

"Oh, thank you!" said Alice gratefully, picking up the tape box and the coffee cup. Should she say how hard she would work to justify Rosa's confidence in her? It seemed presumptuous to pull that reassuring-the-buyer trick again and announce that Rosa had made a wise decision.

Fortunately the phone rang, and Rosa picked it up. "Yes?" she barked, dismissing Alice with a wave and launching into an animated conversation in a foreign language.

In the lobby, the pleasant receptionist had already arranged the application for her on a clipboard and asked Alice if she wanted more coffee. Alice said, "No, thank you," and sat down to fill out the form, reflecting that she'd filled out dozens of them just a few weeks ago, always with a sinking heart and a feeling of doom. This time she dared to be hopeful. If it worked out, she'd have the satisfaction of telling that reptile Judy Livermore that she was going to be working in an office with a nice person at the front desk.

It wasn't until she got into the elevator that it struck her: Rosa Delgado's card had disappeared from her Rolodex! Maybe Chip Gilmore had stolen it along with the catalog! Bowled over by Rosa's direct manner and glamorous appearance, Alice hadn't paid much attention to her ethnicity. She had a Spanish name, but she wasn't speaking Spanish on the phone. Filipinas had Spanish names. Maybe she'd been speaking Tagalog or some other language of the Philippines. And Rosa had told her before that she'd come to America twenty years ago. Had Chip Gilmore stolen her Rolodex card because she was the woman he'd married?

Bob LeBaron said Chip's mail-order bride had gone back to Asia. He'd said Hong Kong, but a lot of those women in the catalog were from the Philippines. Anyway, Bob was pretty vague about Asia. He'd thought Michiko was a Chinese name, for instance.

Chip might have thought his wife had gone back, too, until Ed ran into her while selling ads, and presumably recognized her and blackmailed Ed. And now Chip knew where she was! Chip might try to hurt her. Rosa was living proof he'd married an Asian woman.

Alice started shaking, she was so excited. It was all so clear: Ed had been blackmailing Chip because Rosa was part of his past and was still around. Chip had killed Ed, then searched his papers to see if he could find Rosa and kill her, too. She had to be warned!

Alice jabbed the button for the top floor, but the elevator kept going down. She'd have to go all the way down to the lobby, then start up again. She was hyperventilating now.

As the elevator doors opened onto the lobby she wondered what would happen if she was wrong. Would Rosa think she was crazy and not offer her a job? Maybe Alice should call the police instead. Or maybe there was another way to warn Rosa, a way to phrase it so that if Alice was wrong, she wouldn't sound crazy and full of conspiracy theories. If Rosa had been married to Chip Gilmore, she might not want anybody—especially an employee—to know about her past.

One thing was certain. If Alice told Detective Lukowski and he interrogated Rosa Delgado, Alice could probably kiss her new job good-bye. Rosa didn't seem like the kind of person who would like a prospective employee subjecting her to a police inquiry without warning. Alice stepped out of the elevator and stood there in the lobby as it whooshed back up, empty, to Rosa's floor. She would have to think this through very carefully.

In the car on the way back to KLEG, she decided to send a fax. If she worded it carefully, she could warn Rosa without alarming her in case there was no connection between her and Chip Gilmore. A fax also had the advantage of being one-way communication. Alice was too nervous to get into a conversation with Rosa about her theories. If Rosa had reason to be alarmed, she could call the police herself.

When she pulled up to the station, Alice was flabbergasted to see a big TV news van bristling with satellite dishes parked in front. Now what?

As she went inside, Judy grabbed her sleeve roughly and made a shushing noise. "We're on live TV," she hissed.

Alice looked up and saw a portly man with an outdated silver pompadour facing a young girl with a video camera. He was speaking into a microphone: "Phil Bernard has been in there for several hours now and shows no signs of giving up his vinyl vigil. He's a man who marches to a different drummer, and the rhythm is strictly thirty-three and a third. This is Rex Blaine— and Fluffy—with *Blaine's Byways*. Back to you, Becky and Max."

Over his shoulder, visible through the glass, Phil was making absurd faces, pulling his mouth wide with his forefingers, flapping his tongue and pressing his nose against the glass so it looked like a pig's nose.

Blaine stood there like a robin listening for a worm, touched his earpiece and chuckled into the microphone. "Well, Becky, after all my years on the people beat, I've learned that some folks care deeply about what may seem trivial to the rest of us. But, no, this is apparently not a publicity gimmick."

Instantly, his jovial expression was replaced by one apparently intended to convey compassion. "KLEG personnel have decided that if Phil Bernard doesn't come out of the booth by the end of business today, they'll alert Seattle Mental Health Services, but they're hoping that won't be necessary. We'll keep you updated."

"My God!" said Alice when he'd finished.

"He's flipped out completely," said Judy bitterly.

"Can't we just turn off the station?" demanded Alice.

"I don't know how," said Judy defensively. "It's not really my job. Carl knows how, but he's gone. Bob just keeps ignoring me when I ask him. He and Daphne think being on the news is more important than the dignity of KLEG."

"Well, here's the Delgado Enterprises tape," said Alice, handing her the box. "If things ever get back to normal, rotate the three spots equally."

"Will you help me with the phones?" said Judy in a whiny voice. "We're getting a lot of strange calls."

"I can't. I have to send an important fax," said Alice. She was determined to accomplish that one thing, then get out of this zoo. What was the point of watching poor Phil disintegrate behind the glass? It was hideous. She was already overwrought by the thought that Chip Gilmore might try to kill Rosa Delgado, for heaven's sake!

She went to her desk and tried to ignore the conversation between Bob LeBaron and Rex Blaine behind her. Bob was saying, "Are you going to stick around in case the guys from the funny farm come to take him away?"

"My assignment editor says I can stay for another twenty

minutes or so," said Blaine. "I might get a chance to update with another cut-in."

Alice sat down and wrote her fax:

Dear Ms. Delgado,

I have passed your tape on to our continuity department with instructions to rotate all the spots equally. I appreciate your business and am confident the advertising schedule will produce results for Delgado Enterprises.

Thank you, too, for the opportunity to apply for a sales position with you. I know I would be a highly motivated employee, and I feel strongly that under your direction I can produce good results for your company.

Sincerely,
Alice Jordan
Advertising Sales

P.S.: I thought I should let you know that I have just discovered that your business card is missing from my Rolodex. I mention this because it may have been taken during the break-in I mentioned. The police believe a man named Chip Gilmore went through Ed Costello's papers on my desk. Considering the circumstances, I felt you might want to know. A.J.

She went over to the fax machine and heard Daphne say eagerly to Rex Blaine, "Why don't you interview me? I can say how Phil seemed just fine, then all of a sudden—"

As Alice punched up the number on the fax machine, a small white poodle came over and sniffed her ankle. Startled, she let out a little cry and jumped back. The dog started yapping.

Rex looked over at her. "Oh, she won't hurt you," he said. The dog bared its small but very pointy teeth.

"What is a dog doing here?" asked Alice.

"That's Fluffy," said Rex Blaine indignantly. "Don't you have a TV?"

"Fluffy is Rex's sidekick," explained Bob. "You know, *Blaine's Byways.*"

"I cover the offbeat and unusual. Fluffy adds pizzazz," said Blaine. "Like John Steinbeck and Charlie. It started out as a one-time gag, but everyone loved her so much she's a permanent part of the team. Everyone loves Fluffy."

The camera operator, a rangy young woman in jeans and a sweater, rolled her eyes and said, "Yeah, right."

Alice managed to push the transmit button just before Fluffy darted at her and sank her teeth into her ankle. She screamed. Fluffy, looking pleased with herself, trotted back to Rex Blaine's side, and he patted her. "Bad girl," he said sweetly. Then he glared at Alice as if it were her fault. "She's never done that before," he said.

Behind him, even Phil looked interested, leaning against the glass for a better view, as Alice rubbed her ankle.

"Animals know things instinctively about people," said Judy ominously.

"This is all too much," said Alice, feeling her eyes welling up with tears. Fluffy came back and circled Alice in what looked like a victory lap.

"Is the skin broken?" asked the camera operator. She was wearing heavy shoes and made a kicking motion toward the dog, who beat a retreat. Alice staggered into a chair and examined her ankle. There were little red marks there, and the stocking was ruined, but the skin was intact.

"That damn dog should be put down," said the camera operator. "She's a nasty little thing, and the whole van smells like wet dog all the time." The young woman turned on Rex. "I'm telling the station attorney that we'll have a lawsuit on our hands if we don't get rid of that little bitch."

"Which bitch?" said a lovely voice from the door. They all turned around to see a glamorous woman with long black hair and sunglasses. She wore a red polka-dot dress and a big red straw hat to match. She stood framed in the doorway for just a moment, placing her red-nailed hand against it, and stuck out one hip. They all stared at her in silence; then she sashayed into the reception area.

"I was worried about poor Phil," she said. "I thought I should come down and reason with him."

"That voice!" exclaimed Bob LeBaron.

"Can I help you?" asked Judy, looking confused.

"It's Teresa!" said Daphne.

"I thought it was time you all met me," replied Teresa.

"Wow," said Daphne. "You don't look like what we thought you would at all. We thought you were obese or disfigured or something."

"Hey, here's a little story for you," LeBaron said to Rex Blaine. "This is our mystery lady. No one's ever met her before."

"Come over here, sweetheart," said Blaine. "You'll look great on camera."

"It's a more interesting story than you might think," said Teresa.

Ten minutes later, as the staff stood in a circle, flabbergasted, Blaine was talking into the camera once again. Alice was relieved that he was holding Fluffy. "So there you have it folks. KLEG, the quiet little classical station, turns out to be a pretty wild

196

place. We've just been talking to Teresa, Queen of the Night. For years, she's built up a loyal following of listeners while, unbeknownst to the staff here, Teresa was actually—"

Teresa giggled here and finished his sentence: "Carl Weeb, mild-mannered record librarian."

"Like I say, this is a wild place, Becky and Max. Meanwhile, Carl's boss, the mean old guy who wouldn't let Carl be on the air, is flipping out inside the booth. Who says classical music is dull? This is Rex Blaine—and Fluffy, of course—with *Blaine's Byways*." Teresa patted the dog and smiled into the camera, and Rex gave Fluffy a little pinch so she'd bark good-bye.

"My God, Carl," Bob LeBaron said, "you're a knockout. I never would have guessed." He turned to Rex Blaine and said, "I thought he was straight after that time I found him reading a Victoria's Secret catalog, but I guess he was just ordering a few things."

"Oh, Carl," said Daphne, coming up and giving Teresa a hug. "I've been really jealous of Teresa all this time. But now that I found out she's actually you, I'm so happy. Phil's always treated you badly, and you were always so quiet and patient. I never knew you had such talent and"—she groped for a noun, finally coming up with "self-esteem."

Alice, still massaging her ankle, turned to Judy. "Does Franklin know what's going on around here?"

"Why should we tell him anything?" Judy said unpleasantly. "He doesn't care. He just wants to sell the place."

"I've had a rough day," said Alice to no one in particular. "I'm going home. As soon as I call Franklin."

She limped over to the phone in her cubicle and got Franklin on the line. "I think you should know we have an emergency. I think you should get down here."

"I don't have time for that radio station right now," he said impatiently. "What kind of emergency?"

"Well, Phil went in the booth and started ranting on about vinyl, and then he locked himself in and then—"

Franklin interrupted her. "Hang on a sec," he said. "My secretary is trying to tell me something. What is it, Lois?"

Alice heard Lois very distinctly. Her voice seemed to be coming out of some desktop speaker. "Mr. Ott is here to take you to your Chip Gilmore appointment," she said.

Alice was startled. What was Franklin doing with Chip Gilmore? He'd acted as if he didn't even know the guy.

"Look, Alice," Franklin said, sounding even more irritable than usual, "I've got to go now. I'll check in with the station later. Phil will eventually have to go to the bathroom, won't he? Until then, how bad can it be?"

"All right," said Alice listlessly. She didn't want to prolong the conversation. It would keep her from racking her brain to find some reason Franklin would be consorting with a probably homicidal Nazi.

She'd better call Lukowski. This was all too complicated. She had started to riffle through the phone book, looking for the number to call, when Judy sidled up to her. "You left this in the fax machine," she said coyly, dangling the letter to Rosa over the cubicle wall.

"Thanks," said Alice, wondering if—and hoping that—the events around the station were so extraordinary that Judy might have neglected to read it.

Phil's voice boomed out over the monitor. "God damn you, you bastard, Franklin Payne," he was yelling. "You're the Antichrist." His voice softened back into bland announcer mode.

"And now a violin concerto featuring a very young Yehudi Menuhin, his charming sister Hephzibah at the keyboard."

Alice took malicious pleasure in Phil's latest tirade. "How bad can it be?" Franklin had asked. Now he was being vilified all over town. She sighed and ran her fingers nervously through her hair. She couldn't call the police calmly from here with Phil going literally crazy and Judy probably eavesdropping. She'd have to do it from home.

She folded the memo to Rosa and put it in her purse just as Rex Blaine's camera operator began packing up her equipment. "We've milked this little circus for all it's worth," she said bitterly.

As Alice made her way out the door, a straight-backed, square-jawed man with gray at his temples came bursting through. "Where's Teresa?" he demanded.

Alice pointed over her shoulder and stopped to watch him.

"Teresa," he said, "I saw you on TV."

"Stan!" said Teresa. "I wanted to tell you some other way, about Carl and all—"

"It's all right, sweetheart," he said. "Just a detail that cannot change how I feel. In fact, I think I already knew in some strange way. But when I heard how that Phil wouldn't let you on the air, and all you'd been through, I just wanted to rush right down and be with you."

"Oh, Stan," said Teresa, holding out her hand, which he took between his. "I just thought there was nothing left to lose. They're talking about selling KLEG, and I wanted to go out with a bang."

"How much do they want for it?" asked Stanton.

CHAPTER TWENTY-THREE

When Alice got home, she discovered Zack sprawled on the living room sofa with the portable phone. Lately he'd taken to spending hours talking to his friends, the conversations unintelligible and consisting in large part of sentence fragments like "Cool," "No way," "Just chillin'," and "Wow."

"I need the phone," she said impatiently.

"I gotta go. Mom wants the phone. She never talks long. I'll call you right back."

From the fact that the phone seemed to be body temperature she surmised he'd already been talking for hours.

"Don't you have any homework?" she asked him.

"I can do it in homeroom," he said.

"No phone until it's done," she said, collapsing onto the sofa. Zack went to his room, and she called Lukowski right away.

She left a voice mail message with a detailed description of what she had discovered—Rosa's missing card, her fear that Rosa might be Chip's long-lost mail-order bride and that he might want to harm her, and finally, her theory that Ed Costello might have been killed because he'd found Rosa and was blackmailing Chip Gilmore, ending with "I hope this is helpful," before she put the portable phone down on the coffee table and leaned back, closing her eyes.

She felt a strange mixture of exhaustion and excitement. "No skateboarding in the house," she screamed in the direction of Zack's room where a rumbling sound had been added to the rock music he said he needed to concentrate on his homework.

"Sorry the car's such a mess," said Ron Ott cheerfully. He was throwing some fast-food wrappers over his shoulder into the back seat to make room for Franklin in the front.

Franklin noticed there still seemed to be a lot of french fries on the floor in front of the passenger seat, so he got into the beat-up old station wagon carefully, but still managed to place his black wing tip in the middle of a half-used foil packet of ketchup.

"Has Chip got the money?" asked Franklin as Ott pulled away from the curb.

"Well, it's kind of a long story," said Ott. "But that's okay. It'll take us quite a while to get to Chip's house. He lives way up north."

Franklin let out a deep sigh, and Ott launched into his tale. "The thing is, Chip was married years ago."

"I know," said Franklin. "To some poor little woman he ordered out of a catalog."

"Oh, really?" said Ott. "I never knew how they met. How did you know? Nobody knows about this."

"Never mind," said Franklin. "Go on."

Ott seemed alarmed. "As a public figure, Mr. Gilmore wishes to be very discreet about this marriage. He prefers attention be focused on his message," he said.

"You mean he's embarrassed to be a racist who once married a person of another race?" said Franklin.

"Well, it might be better if you not reveal your knowledge of this marriage when we meet Chip. He's kind of touchy about it."

"Fine," said Franklin, who'd had a youthful marriage he was a little touchy about himself. "What does any of this have to do with his buying KLEG, anyway?"

"His wife went back to Manila after a couple of weeks. At least that's what my client was led to believe. But Ed Costello found out different. He found out she was still in Seattle. And that she has a great deal of money."

"What does this have to do with KLEG?" repeated Franklin.

"Are you aware this is a community-property state?" said Ott with a self-satisfied smirk.

"Of course I am," snapped Franklin. "I'm a lawyer, for God's sake."

"Well, I advised Mr. Gilmore that half of what his wife has is his. They were never divorced. Ed assured us she's worth millions and owns real property all over the state. His share will finance the purchase of KLEG."

"It could take years and years to get that all sorted out," said Franklin. Ott's promising his client millions in what was bound to be a very complicated divorce with a well-financed opponent showed just how stupid he was.

"Mrs. Gilmore is using another name," continued Ott. "What does this suggest to you?"

"That she doesn't want to remember a big mistake," said Franklin.

"I think the immigration authorities might be interested in her," said Ott. "Years ago Chip refused to cooperate when she tried to get a green card on the basis of being married to him."

"Are you telling me that you plan to blackmail this woman?" demanded Franklin.

"No, no," said Ott hastily. "I'm just giving you a little background to let you know that Mr. Gilmore has a rosy financial future. Unfortunately, Ed died before revealing this person's new identity. He was holding out for some kind of a finder's fee. In any case, knowledge of this woman's new name and whereabouts has recently come into Mr. Gilmore's possession, and he contacted her."

Yeah, and he probably got the name and address by breaking into KLEG, thought Franklin. It must have been somewhere in Ed's box.

"Mrs. Gilmore already told my client she'd be willing to settle a large amount on him. I feel sure that when we meet with Mr. Gilmore, he'll report positively on his meeting with Mrs. Gilmore."

"You mean I'm driving all the way up to hell and gone just to see if his wife gave him a check?" said Franklin.

"Frankly, I expected to have heard from Chip by now," said Ott. "But as I've explained before, he's a little eccentric. Anyway, his lieutenants up at the house left a message for me to get up there as soon as possible, so I'm sure we'll have something to discuss. He doesn't like to discuss business on the phone. It is a fact that his activities, all protected under the First Amendment to the Constitution of the United States, may attract the attention of various authorities," added Ott darkly.

Franklin had a vision of the sinister Ghurkas and shadowy United Nations officials of Chip's fevered imagination tapping his phone and listening to him try to shake down his wife.

"Here's the place," said Ott, pulling up in front of a depressing little dingy yellow house. Franklin got out of the car, scraped the ketchup off his shoe on the weedy parking strip and followed Ott up to the porch. The sound of barking dogs from behind a battered old door alarmed him, and then he heard a voice yell, "Who is it?"

"Ron Ott!"

"Password?"

Ron Ott muttered "Triumph" and then gave Franklin an embarrassed, go-figure shrug.

The door opened, and the dogs quieted down. The skinny youths Franklin had first seen in the parking lot of the bad Italian restaurant in West Seattle peered out suspiciously.

"Who's he?" said one of them.

"He has an appointment with Chip," explained Ott. "It's okay. He's with me. This is Franklin Payne. Justin and Brett."

The two dopey-looking kids glanced at each other, then seemed to come to some conclusion.

"Okay," said Justin, the one who had done all the talking. "Come in. There's some pretty bad shit been going down. Our enemies have struck."

"What the hell are you talking about?" demanded Franklin.

Brett burst into a sob. "They killed him. They shot him," he said. "Our leader, Chip, is dead."

"What?" said Ott.

"See for yourself," said the sobbing youth.

Franklin followed Ott through the door into the living room where Chip Gilmore's tubby corpse lay in a Naugahyde BarcaLounger, head back, mouth and eyes open, arms and legs sprawled apart. In the middle of his white T-shirt was a large patch of dark blood. Square in the center of the patch was a large black hole.

"We found him here this morning," said Justin, gnawing on

his cuticles. "We called your office, but it was an unsecured land line, so we just left a message for you to get here real fast. Then some cops came by, but we didn't let them in. Chip always told us to talk to you first."

"I see," said Ott, staring woozily at his dead client before looking away and bracing himself on the wall.

"Brett and me figured they're already working on a way to get the cover-up going," said Justin, narrowing his eyes.

"Yeah," said his companion craftily. "It's no coincidence that the cops show up before they even know he's been killed, right?"

Franklin took in a few of the details in the room. A big old-fashioned television in the corner. Empty beer cans on the coffee table. Bent and grimy venetian blinds. A large still from Leni Riefenstahl's *Triumph of the Will* on the wall.

The thing to do, he thought to himself, was get the hell out of here and call the cops from somewhere else. He did not want to spend time in this dump waiting for the police with one dead sleazebag lunatic, two live ones, a couple of Doberman pinschers and a complete idiot like Ott.

Neither did he want to spend a lot of time being interrogated by detectives at the scene, like when Ed Costello had turned up in that Hide-A-Bed. Just explaining why he was having dealings with these ghastly people would be humiliating enough. He'd rather do it in the dignified surroundings of his own office.

Brett was now saying, "Chip thought this might happen. He was ready to die for the cause. He knew, man. He told us there'd be a cover-up. It's already started. We better not call the cops."

"We'll have to," said a badly shaken Ott. "What else can we do? As your lawyer, I advise you to call the cops right away."

Justin, an aggressive edge to his voice, said, "Not so fast. There's shit around here the cops shouldn't find. We've got to clean it up and do stuff to make sure the cover-up doesn't start right away. Like in that movie about Kennedy."

"Listen," Franklin said mildly. "Maybe I should just go and leave you guys to sort this all out."

"No fucking way," said Justin. "Stay here until we figure out what to do."

"Look," said Franklin firmly. "I'm leaving."

"Forget about it," said Brett. "You heard Justin." Franklin was horrified to see that he had produced a pistol and was pointing it at Franklin.

"Hey, Brett," said Ott in a frightened voice. "As your attorney, I'd advise you to put down the gun."

Brett looked confused.

"The thing is," said Franklin, trying to sound patient and reasonable, "if there is a cover-up, it will be important that you have an impartial witness who left the area and can tell the truth about what happened here." He realized that he was making no sense at all, but counted on the fact that sense was probably the wrong approach to Brett anyway.

Brett turned to Justin and gave him an inquiring look.

"An impartial witness away from the scene, like in Hitler's bunker," Franklin added solemnly, although what Hitler's bunker could possibly have to do with the present situation he couldn't imagine. He was just jabbering, but he tried to give his words some sense of importance.

"Hitler's bunker. Right," said Justin, nodding thoughtfully. "Maybe he's got a point."

Brett lowered the gun, and Franklin, his heart pounding, slowly backed toward the door. Ott looked at him with a pathetic yearning, as if he too would have liked to get the hell out of there.

Then, more terrified than ever now that his back was turned to these gun-toting nutcases, Franklin walked through the front door and down the crumbling concrete path to the street. He turned once, to see the house number so he could give it to the police, and was relieved to see only the two dogs staring at him through the window. Presumably Ott was trying to persuade Brett and Justin to call the cops and to refrain from screwing around with the crime scene in some ditzy attempt to confound imaginary enemies.

A few blocks away, Franklin found a 7-Eleven with a pay phone. He called 911 and told the dispatcher that he, in the company of Ron Ott, had arrived at Gilmore's house and found him shot dead. "There are two vicious-looking dogs and a couple of goofy kids with guns in there, too," added Franklin helpfully. After giving his own name and address, he called a cab.

It arrived just as the sound of police sirens became audible. Franklin got in gratefully, gave the driver his home address and collapsed against the back of the seat, closing his eyes. He'd been through the most hellish experience of his life, and all because of that damn radio station.

The driver turned around and said to him, "Mind if I keep the radio on? There's weird stuff happening at this funky little AM classical station. This guy locked himself in the studio and he's going crazy."

"Why not," said Franklin, feeling completely defeated. Hadn't Alice Jordan told him something about Phil going berserk? Apparently his ranting was interesting enough to the cabdriver.

With a snicker, the driver turned up the volume.

Franklin flinched as the sound of Phil's voice filled the cab. "This is Classic KLEG on your AM dial," he said. "Franklin

Payne, if you're listening, remember you have precipitated a terrible crisis. You are responsible."

"Oh, my God," said Franklin.

"He seems to have it in for this Payne character," explained the driver. "This is pretty wild stuff."

"In fact," Phil went on, "it is a crisis of global proportions. It is time to open the red envelope."

"Not the red envelope!" said Franklin.

"What?" said the driver.

"Forget about the address I just gave you," said Franklin. "I want you to take me to that radio station."

CHAPTER TWENTY-FOUR

"What's he doing now?" asked Daphne, squinting through the studio window.

"Oh, my God," said Judy. "He's messing around with the EBS file."

"What's that?" asked Stanton Edgecombe.

Teresa put a hand on his arm. "The Emergency Broadcast System. We're only supposed to open the red envelope in case some government authorities call and say there's some huge disaster. The red envelope has codes in it, so we know we're talking to some legit authority. That way, cranks can't call up and say a volcano is about to erupt or something."

"Here it is!" announced Phil wildly. He pulled out a sheaf of papers, looked puzzled for a moment, flung a few of them to one side and then shouted, "Yes! Tango Romeo Bravo Whiskey!"

He pushed his glasses up his nose and grabbed a large booklet. "We interrupt our program at the request of the White House," he began in agitated tones. "This is the Emergency Broadcast System. All normal broadcasting has been discontinued during this emergency. This is KLEG-AM. This station will continue to broadcast, furnishing news, official information and instructions for the Seattle area as soon as possible."

"We better shut him down," said Bob in grave tones. "There could be huge FCC fines involved. In all my days in broadcasting, I've never heard of anyone messing with the EBS stuff."

"The civilian population could be alarmed," said Stanton Edgecombe. "We can't shut him down without an explanation in mid-broadcast. We've got to get in there."

Phil was still reading: "Do not use the telephone. The telephone lines should be kept open for official use."

Stanton Edgecombe examined the door hinges.

Phil, after rummaging around some more in the EBS file, segued neatly from the White House message to another booklet, this one a yellowed old relic.

"Oh, my God," said Teresa. "He's got ahold of that funky old civil defense brochure from the fifties. We should have cleaned that file out years ago."

Outside the building, Franklin threw some money at the cabdriver and ran into the station just as Phil was saying, "Warheads are aimed at Seattle. Remain calm. Proceed in an orderly fashion to your nearest civil defense air-raid shelter as soon as possible. Authorities will give you further instructions there. If you do not know where your nearest air-raid shelter is, prepare basements and cellars with food and potable water for seven days, blankets, and battery-operated radio receivers. An all clear will sound when the highest danger of radiation poisoning has passed. This is not a test. This is an actual emergency. If you are at home when the blast comes, stay away from windows, as the blast will shatter them."

"You're damn right it will," said an enraged Franklin. Picking up an office chair, he shouted, "Stand back!" and proceeded to-ward the glass at a fast clip, carrying the chair over his head.

"I wonder how things are going at the station," said Caroline, sipping her first margarita of the day and leaning back in her lounger next to the pool. "I haven't had the heart to call and find out, but with Franklin in charge, I suppose everything will be running smoothly." A light breeze riffled the palm fronds far above her head.

"How much do you think KLEG is worth?" asked Jeffrey in the lounger beside hers. Like Caroline, he was wearing a swim-suit, sunglasses and glistening sunblock.

"Oh, I don't know. Lots and lots, Franklin says. I feel like a rat deserting KLEG, but you've convinced me that I must think of myself for a change. I need to make my mark as my own per-son, not as an extension of Mama."

"Exactly," said Jeffrey.

"Besides," she said, smiling fondly at him, "I made the deci-sion to keep KLEG going before I knew I'd meet you. All my priorities have changed, darling."

"Why don't you call your brother and tell him?" said Jeffrey. "Maybe he can unload the thing right away, send you a check, and we can get started on the rest of our lives." He leaned over, removed his sunglasses, kissed her and said fervently, "Oh, my darling, I'm such a lucky man."

A few minutes later, a waiter had brought them fresh marga-ritas and plugged a phone into a convenient jack cunningly fit-ted into the border around the patio. A call to Franklin's office elicited the information that he was at KLEG, having just called in from there to collect messages.

The phone at the station rang about fifteen times before Judy, sounding very frazzled, answered it, and passed her over to Franklin.

Franklin was calmer now. The straight-backed, take-charge man, whom Franklin didn't know but who he thought might be from the FCC, had had a good idea when he suggested that they crisscross the studio window with masking tape before smashing it. The tape had prevented Phil from being injured by flying glass, although at the moment of impact, Franklin hadn't worried too much about Phil's safety, filled as he was with rage.

The take-charge guy had then climbed in the studio window, pried the two-by-fours loose quickly with the hammer, and opened the door. The good-looking woman with him had rushed in and taken the microphone to tell the world that nuclear war had not—repeat, had not—broken out, that Phil Bernard would be taking a very long rest in quiet surroundings, and that KLEG apologized for any inconvenience the bogus announcement of Armageddon might have caused its listeners.

A call to 911 produced not the legendary men in white coats with stretcher but a mousy social worker type, a young man in socks and sandals, who chatted quietly with Phil, pronounced him delusional, and arranged for some medics to take him to Harborview Hospital for overnight observation.

Listening to the woman on the air, Franklin realized they had finally found the mysterious Teresa. She was a stunner all right, but Franklin didn't care for her flashy clothes and overdone makeup. In person, she looked as trampy as her patter sounded.

"And now," she concluded, "what could be more soothing after such an intense afternoon than something lush and sensual? If you were unnerved by Phil Bernard's unfortunate delusions, and we all wish him well in the future, sit back, relax and bathe yourself in the music of Dvořák."

When she came out of the booth a moment later, Franklin confronted her. "Listen, Teresa, I'm glad to finally meet you, but we'll have to have a talk. Recording that message for Ed Costello's escort service didn't do the station much good. It's a question of loyalty and judgment. And I'd also like to talk about your compensation. We have to make sure our records with the IRS are clear." As he scolded her, Franklin had the strange feeling he had met Teresa before.

She ignored his tirade and slipped her arm into that of the tall man beside her. "This is Stanton Edgecombe. He has a question for you. Can we step into your office?"

Franklin escorted them in and slid the glass door closed. The men stood while Teresa sat down and fussed with her hemline over her smooth young knees.

"Thanks for your help," Franklin said to Edgecombe as they both sat. "Things were definitely out of control."

"This place needs new management," declared Stanton Edgecombe. "Teresa thinks you're willing to sell. How much do you want for KLEG?"

"Half a million," said Franklin eagerly. Although with some encouragement, he'd have been willing to sign the whole thing over for a dollar.

Stanton looked thoughtful. "Five hundred thousand. That sounds doable," he said. "I've just inherited my mother's house in San Francisco. It's worth twice that. I'd like Teresa here to have complete managerial and creative control. I don't know anything about broadcasting, I just know what I like." He turned and beamed at her.

There was a scrabbling noise at the door. Judy was wheezing at the latch.

Franklin slid the door open a crack. "What?" he asked irritably.

"Here are some weird papers from the studio," said Judy. "I saw Phil take them out of the red envelope. They don't have anything to do with the Emergency Broadcast System."

"All right," said Franklin, grabbing them and flinging them on the desk. "Could you leave us alone, please? We have something important to discuss."

"There's also this," said Judy with a grim little smile. "I found it in the fax machine. I Xeroxed it because I thought you should know that Alice Jordan is looking for another job. It says so right here."

"Thank you!" shouted Franklin, trying to slide the door shut. What an idiot that Judy was! He'd told them all to get real and look for new jobs. Alice Jordan had had the initiative to do so, and now Judy tried to make a big deal of it! He managed to get the door closed, his hand being quicker than the foot that she tried to insert in the doorway.

"That woman is a real piece of work," he said, shaking his head.

"If I have anything to say about it, she'll be the first one out the door," said Teresa, lifting an eyebrow.

"Good move," said Franklin.

Now Judy was banging on the glass again. He slid the door open and said, "What is it?" in a near bellow.

"Your sister's on line two," said Judy.

"I'd better take this call," he said. What if Caroline came back before he could arrange a sale to this Edgecombe character? He'd encourage her to stay away for as long as it took to nail down the deal.

"Hi, Caroline," he said in a soothing voice. "Having a good time? God knows, you deserve it."

"Everything's great. How are things at KLEG?"

"Oh, fine," he said vaguely. Why distress her with Phil's on-air psychotic break and the legal problems that would doubtless follow? She might think she was needed and come back.

"I'll come straight to the point, Franklin," she said. "I feel I'm ready for new challenges. I'm thinking maybe we should sell KLEG."

"Fine," said Franklin in a calm voice, although his heart was leaping with delight. "I'll get on it right away."

"Let me tell you how my thinking evolved on this," said Caroline dreamily. "You see, I always felt left out, even as a girl, because Mama never let me do anything."

Franklin murmured "Uh-huh" and made a finger-twirling, eye-rolling gesture of impatience in the direction of Edgecombe and Teresa to indicate he'd try and get off the phone soon. The gesture was wasted on them, however, as they were gazing soulfully into each other's eyes.

"I think my feelings of disempowerment were tied up with KLEG," said Caroline. "Jeffrey has explained it all to me and encouraged me to get out from under my responsibilities there."

Franklin said, "I understand," and, from long habit, tuned her out, glancing down at the desk in front of him, where his eye struck the papers Judy had delivered.

"It's an esteem thing, Franklin. I'm afraid I've always felt that you didn't respect me, either."

"Yeah, that's right," he said, scanning the documents with growing excitement. It was clear to him that someone—almost certainly Ed Costello—had found a very clever place to hide things.

Sly old Ed had probably steamed open the EBS envelope, put the stuff in and glued the flap back down, assuming the documents would never be found unless a tidal wave, earthquake or nuclear attack was imminent, in which case no one would pay too much attention to them. Ed hadn't counted on Phil's going off his rocker.

Caroline was still maundering on about herself. "I'm afraid you've never listened to me. Really listened."

"Absolutely, okay, great, gotta go," said Franklin hastily, hanging up on her. The police should see this stuff right away. The documents included a marriage license in the names of Charles Gilmore and one Lourdes Contreras, a photocopy of a wedding picture of Chip and his diminutive bride, a news clipping about a women entrepreneurs' banquet with a picture of Rosa Delgado that strongly resembled Chip's wife in the wedding shot. There was also a note in Ed's handwriting that said simply, "Rosa Delgado = Lourdes's cousin. Green card switch? INS? Community property." Beside this was a row of dollar signs, much like the ones on the Post-it note bearing Chip Gilmore's phone number.

Franklin turned to Stanton Edgecombe and Teresa, said he'd talk to them later and repeated his desire to sell the station as soon as possible. Stan gave him a firm handshake, and they left.

While Franklin was on hold waiting for Lukowski, he checked out more of the documents that had been hidden in the red envelope. They included a computer diskette marked very neatly "Home Run Records." Franklin assumed these weren't major-league stats but the books for the escort service. There was also an envelope with Jeffrey Fleming's name on it. Could this be Caroline's new boyfriend?

Franklin opened it up and found a small item from a newspaper, which he read with interest. An underage high school gymnast. Porn shots. And a jury verdict that took twenty minutes. Caroline sure knew how to pick them.

There were also some prints of the shots in question. As he studied the pictures, the speed of the jury verdict became obvious. Franklin amused himself on hold by trying to decide which girl in the artfully constructed tableau was underage and also whether anyone other than a trained gymnast could do what these girls were doing.

Lukowski finally came on the line, and Franklin described what he'd found. Lukowski said he'd come by the station as soon as he could to pick up the items.

Before he did, Franklin went over to the Xerox machine and made copies of the Jeffrey Fleming materials. For now Fleming was a good influence on Caroline, apparently having persuaded her to sell KLEG. But if he ever became a problem, and Franklin felt sure he would, Franklin would be ready.

Judy came over to him while he was at the copier. He quickly positioned himself so she couldn't see the nubile naked gymnasts picture rolling out of the machine. "What is it now?" he demanded.

"Did you get a chance to read that memo of Alice Jordan's I intercepted?" she asked. "I really question the wisdom of allowing an unmotivated employee to represent the station on a sales basis."

"Oh, for God's sake," said Franklin, "what business is it of yours anyway? You know what? I may be about to sell the station to a guy who's going to let Teresa, Queen of the Night, run the place. She can deal with you and your delusions of grandeur."

"Carl? Carl's going to run the station?" Judy looked alarmed.

"No, not Carl," said Franklin, exasperated. "Teresa!"

Judy just stared at him, and Franklin's eyes grew wide, too, with the dawning realization. Yes, Teresa had looked familiar. Why hadn't he seen it? Once you knew, it was so obvious.

He grabbed Judy's shoulders in an agitated manner. "Does this Stanton Edgecombe know Teresa's a guy?" he demanded. Franklin didn't want Edgecombe to lose interest in his new protégé, and therefore in buying KLEG. Suddenly Franklin realized with revulsion that he was touching Judy.

He quickly let go, and she said, "Sure, he does. Everyone knows. It was on the afternoon news. Didn't you know? They did a live TV broadcast from here showing Phil cracking up. Then Carl showed up in a dress and explained how he was really Teresa."

Great, thought Franklin, wondering how he'd missed that little circus. It must have happened while he was talking his way out of a nest of Nazis, hoping he wouldn't be shot. It had certainly been an eventful day.

He whisked his copies away from Judy's prying eyes and went back to Caroline's office, then collapsed in the chair, exhausted.

He supposed he should wait for Lukowski. And he imagined he'd have to face a lot of irritating questions in the investigation of Chip's murder, too. After all, he was the one who'd made the call to 911.

Idly he picked up the Alice Jordan memo and skimmed it. Too bad she hadn't been around this afternoon. She was always so calm and pleasant, compared to the other employees. She made Franklin feel calm, too.

When he got to the P.S., though, in which Alice warned Rosa Delgado that Chip knew where she was, he sat bolt upright. Somehow Alice Jordan had stumbled onto Chip's wife, too!

Franklin frowned. This was not good news. Franklin had heard Ott's sordid plans for Chip to shake down his estranged wife. Franklin had seen Chip's body and had immediately been struck by the fact that the estranged wife had a clear motive to blow away Chip. Franklin had also seen Ed Costello's body. The bullet holes in the two corpses had looked remarkably similar. Franklin had also discovered Ed's file on Rosa Delgado, who might really be Lourdes Gilmore. Rosa Delgado also had a motive to blow Ed away.

And now that sweet Alice Jordan, simply trying to be helpful, had announced to Rosa Delgado that she had established a link between Rosa and Chip Gilmore. Not only that but she'd applied for a job with her. Rosa Delgado presumably had her address.

Maybe he was jumping to conclusions, but considering the circumstances, Franklin felt the least he could do was get in touch with Alice and tell her to be careful. After all, two people who'd established the same link she had were now dead.

CHAPTER TWENTY-FIVE

When the portable phone on the coffee table rang, Alice hoped it might be Detective Lukowski. She fantasized his calling to tell her she had cleverly solved the murder of Ed Costello, that Chip Gilmore was in custody and had broken down and made a full confession. Instead, to her surprise, the caller was Rosa Delgado.

"Hi, Alice," she said. "I got your fax. I was interested in your P.S. about Charles Gilmore."

"Oh," said Alice offhandedly, "I just thought I should mention it. As a courtesy."

"Did you mention it to anyone else?" asked Rosa.

Alice, despite the fact that Rosa had praised her honest face, decided instantaneously to lie. For some reason Rosa sounded displeased with the possibility Alice had mentioned the missing card to someone else. Alice didn't want to jeopardize her job. "No, I didn't," she said.

"Good," said Rosa. This struck Alice as more than a little odd.

"You see," Rosa went on, "this Gilmore fellow was once married to my cousin Lourdes. He was a horrible man, and there was a big scandal in my family."

"Oh, I see," said Alice, who didn't quite.

"The Philippines is a Catholic country," said Rosa. "Divorce is a very bad thing there. We all want to forget about it. She has a nice new husband and four kids. If the fact that she was divorced gets back to Manila somehow, it could hurt all of them.

"And besides, I don't want anyone to know my family was associated with this man. I have a professional reputation to uphold. I hope I can count on your discretion."

"Of course," said Alice. Didn't Rosa know she might be in danger? Alice felt morally compelled to suggest that possibility. "I only mentioned it because I thought you might be in danger from him. I thought maybe *you* were his ex-wife," she said. "I think Chip Gilmore might have murdered Ed." Alice hoped to God she wouldn't have to explain that Chip was ashamed of having married someone he perceived as from an inferior race. That would be too awful to go into.

There was a long pause. "This sounds serious," said Rosa. "I will handle this. I will call the police. I just hope I can keep our family out of it."

"All right," said Alice, now nervous that Rosa would find out that Alice had already told the police and lied to her. It seemed so unfair. Alice never lied, and now that she finally had, she might be caught and lose a chance at a decent job.

When she hung up, she stretched out full length on the sofa, tense and worried.

The sound of Zack's skateboard started up again. "Homework. No skateboarding," she said wearily. "And not in the house." He had careened down the hall from his room to the slate-covered entry, one of his favorite runs.

She heard a loud clack as he got off the skateboard and pressed one end down with his toe to stop it. Then Zack appeared carrying the board under his arm. He didn't seem to notice she was prostrate with nerves.

"I finished my homework," he said. "I need the phone."

She pointed vaguely in its direction, and he grabbed the phone and scampered off to his room. "When can I have my own phone line?" he asked her over his shoulder.

"Never," she said weakly. "Stop asking for things. There are only two of us. I'm sure we can share it."

Franklin had been trying to call Alice's house for twenty-five minutes, eventually finding himself hitting redial over and over again, only to get a persistent busy signal. He wondered if he was being hysterical. He had a horrible vision of poor Alice, shot dead, with the phone off the hook and a recording saying, "If you want to make a call, hang up," bleating into the stillness.

With a sigh, he flipped through Caroline's address file and discovered where Alice lived. It was a twenty-minute drive. Maybe he should just go over there.

He bundled up the documents Lukowski was coming to get, adding a note that said, "I am at Alice Jordan's. She may be in danger from Rosa Delgado. Her phone's been busy for half an hour, so I've gone to warn her in person." He put everything in a big envelope, sealed it, then delivered it to Judy.

"Give this to Detective Lukowski when he comes," he said. "And don't even think about opening it and snooping like you always do. It contains evidence. If you tamper with it, I'll personally do everything I can to have you arrested and convicted of something. Is that clear?"

To his satisfaction, Judy actually looked frightened. He'd seen fear in her eyes only once before, just a few minutes ago when she'd learned she might be working for Carl.

＊　　＊　　＊

To calm herself down, Alice turned on the television. She kept wondering what Franklin Payne had to do with Chip Gilmore. She couldn't believe he was a secret Nazi. Maybe some news would distract her, but she avoided the channel Rex Blaine and Fluffy worked for. She couldn't bear to see anything about KLEG.

She was arranging some cushions behind her back when the doorbell rang. Probably some friend of Zack's, she thought, dragging herself wearily up from the sofa.

She had arrived at the entry and was opening the door when she heard an announcer on television say, "Police have no suspect as yet in the shooting death of white supremacist Charles Gilmore in his North End home."

She was stunned. Chip Gilmore, who she'd thought was Ed's killer, was now dead himself. What did this mean?

She opened the door. Rosa stood there, pointing a huge gun at her. "Get inside," she said in a hoarse whisper.

"But I don't understand," said Alice, beginning to cry.

"I'm sorry about this," said Rosa fretfully. "You aren't bad, like Chip and Ed. But you found out too much. I'm very sorry, Alice. You would have been a good salesperson."

"But you won't get away with this," said Alice, hoping to God Zack would stay in his room. Would this madwoman kill him, too, if he stumbled into the scene? "You see, I already told the police about you and Chip. So if you kill me they'll know it's you."

"Sorry, Alice," said Rosa sadly. "I don't believe you. You're a bad liar. You told me the truth the first time, when I called. You're an honest person. You didn't tell the police."

"But *I* did," said a man's voice behind Rosa. It was Franklin

Payne's voice. "I told the police. They know about you, Rosa. I told them you might try to hurt Alice."

Rosa's face took on a panicky expression, and she turned sideways and stepped back so she was at right angles to both Alice and Franklin, with her back to the hall. She held her gun at waist height and moved it back and forth in a small arc. In this position, she could shoot either of them.

"You're lying," she said. "No one told the police about me."

Another man's voice came from behind Franklin. It was Detective Lukowski's voice. "Actually, they both told me, Rosa. Put down the gun." He sounded so calm and firm, Alice was sure Rosa would obey. Instead the hand with the gun in it started shaking. "It's not fair," she said.

"I know," said Lukowski from the porch. "But it will be easier for you if you put down the gun. Just set it down on the floor with the barrel pointing away from everyone. We don't want anyone hurt. We know that you're really Lourdes—that Rosa Delgado is the name of a cousin, and you used her green card. You can't pretend anymore."

"The hell with all of you," Rosa screamed, and brought her other hand up to steady the gun. She closed her eyes tight as if she were preparing for a heavy recoil.

"Get down!" shouted Lukowski.

Alice heard the rumble of the skateboard for just a second before Zack came careening down the hall and into the entry. The tip of his board caught Rosa in the back of her ankles, and she tumbled over with a scream. Her heavy gun went flying and slid across the slate entryway.

By the time Zack had scrambled to his feet, Lukowski and Franklin Payne were both on top of Rosa, holding her down.

Alice walked over to where the gun was and nudged it very

carefully across the room with her foot so that Rosa couldn't reach it even if she managed to break free from the two men. Then she wrapped her arms around Zack and held him tightly.

Rosa Delgado lay on the slate floor of the entryway, her hands fastened behind her with plastic cuffs. Lukowski walked over to the gun and smiled. "A Glock."

"Think it will tie in with the two murders?" said Alice, thrilled.

"I sure hope so," he said with a big smile. "You're going to jail," he said to Rosa.

"You saved my life," said Alice to Franklin.

"What's going on?" Zack asked his mother.

"That's the second time today someone's pulled a gun on me," said Franklin to Alice. "Aren't you going to invite me in and offer me a drink?"

Later, after Lukowski had finally left and Rosa had been hauled away, after Zack had been told just what had happened and had rushed off with the phone to his room to tell all his friends, Alice and Franklin sat side by side on the sofa, drinking the last of Ken's expensive Scotch.

"I had it all wrong," said Alice. "I thought Ed was blackmailing Chip. Instead, he was blackmailing Rosa."

"According to Ron Ott," Franklin said, "Ed started out trying to get a finder's fee out of Chip. Chip wanted to buy KLEG, and Costello knew where he could get some money—from the woman Chip had never divorced. But then I think Ed decided he could do better blackmailing Rosa. She had deeper pockets. And not only did she want to keep all her money and not share it with Chip, she was probably in this country illegally. Ott told me Chip worked hard to keep her from getting a green card on the basis of their flimsy little marriage."

"If I'd known that Rosa was an illegal immigrant, I might have figured it all out," said Alice. "I have to admit that I wanted to. It sounds so childish, but the truth is, nothing fascinates me more than crime. I was always a real junkie for this true crime stuff. I've fantasized about investigating things all my life."

"Really?" said Franklin. "Our firm is talking about hiring an assistant for our in-house investigator. It's not all criminal work, though. There's some civil stuff, too. You know—getting pictures of people jumping up and down on trampolines after filing personal-injury suits."

"Oh, that sounds wonderful," said Alice. "Do you think I have a chance?"

"Of course you do," said Franklin. "I'll see to it. And when you're an employee we can get one of our divorce attorneys to go after that wretched ex-husband of yours and his cult."

"My God, you've already done so much for me," she said, her eyes filling with grateful tears. "You saved me from that horrible woman! It was wonderful."

She realized she was holding his hand, and she was even more astonished to find herself collapsing against his shoulder while he patted her on the back.

Zack came into the room, and they pulled apart hastily. "Wow, that Porsche out in front must have set you back a lot," he said. "That's a really cool car!"

"Zack!" said Alice, horribly embarrassed. "That's a terrible thing to say."

Franklin laughed. "It doesn't hurt to know how much things cost," he said. "As long as you don't know the price of everything and the value of nothing. Actually, I think that's probably Rosa Delgado's car."

Zack looked a little disappointed, but then perked up and

said, "Wow. Then yours must be the vintage Mercedes. It's great too, and the value will just go up, right?"

"That's right," said Franklin.

"Well, I'll leave you two alone now. Great car, Mr. Payne," said Zack. "Good night."

"Nice kid," said Franklin.